CRY OF
HORNBILL

Husna is a writer from Kochi, Kerala. She is a dentist by qualification and also has a PG diploma in journalism. She has worked as a content writer for online brands and as feature writer for news portals.

Husna is a published author and poet. Her works include *My Lyrical Symphony* and *Zikr* in poetry, and *Saudade* and *Red River Rising* in fiction.

Instagram: https://www.instagram.com/writer_husna?igsh=Y3k3MGMzdmcydXBl
Facebook: https://www.facebook.com/HusnaAuthor?mibextid=ZbWKwL

CRY OF THE HORNBILL

HUSNA

RUPA

Published by
Rupa Publications India Pvt. Ltd 2025
7/16, Ansari Road, Daryaganj
New Delhi 110002

Sales centres:
Bengaluru Chennai
Hyderabad Jaipur Kathmandu
Kolkata Mumbai Prayagraj

Copyright © Husna 2025

This is a work of fiction. Names, characters, places and incidents are either the product of the author's imagination or are used fictitiously and any resemblance to any actual person, living or dead, events or locales is entirely coincidental.

All rights reserved.
No part of this publication may be reproduced, transmitted or stored in a retrieval system, in any form or by any means, electronic, mechanical, photocopying, recording or otherwise, without the prior permission of the publisher.

P-ISBN: 978-93-6156-765-0
E-ISBN: 978-93-6156-033-0

First impression 2025

10 9 8 7 6 5 4 3 2 1

The moral right of the author has been asserted.

Printed in India

This book is sold subject to the condition that it shall not, by way of trade or otherwise, be lent, resold, hired out, or otherwise circulated, without the publisher's prior consent, in any form of binding or cover other than that in which it is published.

*'You broke the ocean in half to be here.
Only to meet nothing that wants you.'*

—Nayyirah Waheed

Contents

Prologue: The Beginning of an End / ix

The Book of Exodus / 1
The Book of Intrigue / 85
The Book of Mortality / 135

Epilogue / 210

Prologue
The Beginning of an End

The supermoon that December night adorned the city of Kohima like a *jhumar* on a bejewelled bride. It took up a large portion of the sky, like a giant nacre ring suspended in air, making the stars obsolete. From a distance, you could not help but marvel at the stunning backdrop to an unfolding noir film. The night was still young. Sunset was around 5.00 p.m., but on days like this, even twilight seemed endless. The peculiar lunar phenomenon, however, was a facade. If you looked at it long enough, it would trick you into thinking that you could climb the distant hill across the valley and simply reach out for it. *Noor*, as they called the moon sometimes, looked stunning—maleficently so, tonight. A large halo around the hill and a shade of white silver that didn't yet have a name, which was just as well because anything so viscerally stunning leaves you speechless. The dichotomy of language is, one would think, that it is at times excessive and at others, not enough.

For the Nagas of Nagaland, however, it was the perfect time to host the Hornbill Festival, which saw the congregation of culture, history and photography enthusiasts from across the globe. It was known as the 'festival of festivals' for a reason. Ten days of cultural showcasing, during which sixteen dominant Naga tribes put on a spectacular show of their art, heritage and music. The government introduced the festival to promote intertribal relations and tourism. This was also the only way the older generation could pass on the memories of the past, including the glorious days of head-hunting, to the younger ones. A tradition that was reduced to legend and folklore these days.

The world had finally woken up to the vibrant Naga culture, as it often eventually did in the case of indigenous tourism. They hailed Nagaland, which until now had been completely ignored due to the insurgency and civil unrest, as one of the most culturally diverse places on the planet. Tweets, Instagram feeds and Facebook live stories were flooded with colourful pictures of different tribes in their traditional attire and hornbill-feather headwear. If you were lucky, you could take a picture or two featuring octogenarian Konyaks—the last surviving original head-hunters, identified by skull or head chains around their necks, signifying the number of heads they had taken. During these nights of endless celebrations, Kohima took on an almost mystical, fantastical aura. It was no surprise, therefore, why tourists kept coming back for more. Some even stayed longer on projects focusing on the traditional Naga way of life.

But development hadn't kept pace with the influx of tourism. Roads were mostly kutcha. Hotels were too small, lacking frills and ruffles. The next best option was regular homestays. But no one complained about the lack of luxury. Authenticity was the new hallmark of travelling. And this indigenousness—the pristine wilderness in the area—was exactly what the state government wished to market. Nagaland had, thus, become the epitome of untouched virginity.

The need to resurrect itself economically and politically came in the aftermath of the 2014 elections when a new right-wing government came to power in India and reached out to Nagaland to give up the insurgency and join mainstream governance. Nagaland had had one of the longest-running insurgencies in the world, spanning six decades, for independence from the Indian state. It took a lot of negotiations and talks with the various tribes and rebel groups to bring the cycle of violence to a close. It took the British Empire fifty years to subdue the highland, and the Indian government spent another sixty in achieving a reconciliation with its people. The Nagas' aversion to external governance and their demand for the right to self-determination were at the crux of the ceasefire.

But these days, there was a serene sense of order, buoyancy and calm that seemed like it was here to stay. People wanted to forget their turbulent past and move on with their lives. There was an air of hope for a better life. What was freedom, anyway, without economic independence? With decades of insurgency, hardly any development had happened in the state. But now things were looking up. Nagaland would finally find its spot under the sun. And the Hornbill Festival was yet another opportunity for the people of the region to showcase their proud heritage. Hence, it was with much-renewed fanfare and excitement that the ten-day affair was scheduled that year, from 1 December to 10 December.

Kohima was aglow with a spectacular radiance that night. The hills were illuminated by a thousand lights, the supermoon being the centrepiece. The sound of the log drums reverberated through the air. The hypnotic beats were in perfect synchrony. The participants were grouping themselves into different Naga tribes from various regions and as they began the inaugural march, many were already singing the war cry in a menacing tenor. Intermittently, the grunting cry of the hornbill, as though its nest were in danger, broke the sound of the drums and songs. It was an ominous sign of things to come.

At Camp Kismar, on the west end of the festival location, a lone light was on in one of the tents. It was still too early for the campers to return from the inaugural celebrations. Usually around 8.00 p.m., they would light up the campfire and various tour groups would huddle around it for small talk, singing and fellowship. Kohima and the outskirts were a favoured destination amongst bikers and trekkers. They came from different parts of India, as well as from other countries, to experience Naga hospitality. Camp Kismar was the ideal stopover for those who loved outdoor life. The amenities were bare minimum. Around 50 tents were pitched at different levels of the hill with scenic views of the valley and the sky at night. There were those who came every year just for the views. And it was all just walking distance from the festival.

However, on that eventful night, fate had a different plan. Lives changed, lines were redrawn, constellations seemed to merge with each other, as the cry of the hornbill got more desperate. In the far corner of the site, the grass outside one of the tents was turning crimson. The guard who walked past it didn't think much of it until the vermilion trail was forging its path alongside the tent. At first, he mistook it for colour or even paint; on closer inspection, he found that it wasn't either. He called out to make sure all was well. No one answered. Feeling a bit unsettled, he opened the tent. What he next saw knocked the wind out of his lungs. As he let out a deathly scream, the silence of the night was broken a second time.

1

The Book of Exodus

Reality is right here, right now.
All else is illusion.

1

The spotlight was on Camp Kismar. There was a lot of commotion in the middle of the night. The police, along with a few soldiers from the army headquarters, had swarmed the perimeter, anticipating a law-and-order crisis. In Kohima, one never knew what could trigger violence. News had travelled fast and a lot of people, both locals as well as tourists, thronged the camp to find out about the incident. Inspector John Angami furrowed his brows in irritation. It was close to midnight, and he was looking forward to a good night's sleep after a tiresome trip from Imphal. But it seemed as if it was going to be a long night. The first thing he wanted to do was to secure the crime scene. There were just too many people and nosy journalists crowding the area. In the past, many an investigation had been derailed on account of neglecting this detail, which often resulted in crucial evidence getting contaminated.

The victim was identified as Tanya Singh, a photojournalist from Mumbai who was working with *India Times*. Her name was synonymous with investigative journalism and both politicians and the parallel economy mafias had her on their watchlist. She had come to Kohima to investigate the alleged detention and deportation of the Rohingya refugees back to Myanmar after the riots in Dimapur. She was also working in close collaboration with the UNHCR and the external affairs ministry in persuading India to be a signatory to the UN Refugee Convention.

Tanya Singh had worked closely with a family of three refugee sisters on a documentary. She had checked into the camp with a certain Mr Aman Kumar, her ex-boyfriend. He was a tall, attractive man, with a distinct mandala tattoo on his arm. The man with the tattoo had become the talk of the town. Many even wondered if he had his roots in one of the tribes, given the intricacy of the tattoo.

Aman Kumar, as Inspector John Angami learnt, was a hippie sort who was working with an NGO that was run by Ram Nair, a politician with a dubious reputation. He and Tanya had first met while on a vacation in Kerala. They couldn't have been more different. She was the aggressive, no-nonsense firebrand photojournalist from Delhi. And he, a happy-go-lucky kind of guy from Kerala.

The gruesomeness of the murder, however, was what disturbed Angami. It indicated to him that the killer was extremely dangerous and vengeful. The inspector examined the scene of crime closely. He felt a sense of despair looking at the 5'6" tall, beautiful woman lying in a pool of blood before him. The murder had taken place inside the tent. She must have been caught unawares, as there seemed to be no sign of a struggle. There were, however, marks on her wrists and neck. But all those details paled in comparison to what actually caused her death. The partial decapitation. The neck was partially dismembered from the body. He could almost see the tracheal bones. The incision was perfect, but the work was left half-done. Perhaps the weapon wasn't sharp enough. Or perhaps the killer just lost his nerve. There was massive blood loss, as is the case with arterial traumas. It was like a carnage, with blood splashed across the tent and the ground.

Angami kept studying her face. Even in this brutality, there was such serenity about her. Tanya Singh had held so much promise. For the world, humanity, refugee rehabilitation programmes and much more. He was sure that like him, she too probably wanted to change the world in whichever ways she could and fight the system to her best capacity. Only, the system always got the upper hand. Had she lived longer and become older, she would have resigned herself to a cynical detachment like he had. Everyone did after a while. It was a battle too hard to win.

Angami began noting down the details of the crime.

TOD (time of death): Between 9.30 p.m. and 10.00 p.m., give or take a few minutes.

The victim's layered clothing suggested that she had been out, probably at the festival venue, and might have returned just in time for dinner. The shoes were still on.

There was no sign of struggle, which meant the attacker either caught her off guard or was someone she knew.

The precision of the wound was surprising. The cut, almost like a surgical incision, from the left ear to the throat suggested clinical expertise. The jugular was the target area for maximum bleeding.

The depth of the cut suggested an even more sinister motive, as though the attacker wanted to separate the head from the body but couldn't quite bring themselves to complete the task, leaving it halfway. It reminded Angami of the stories he had heard as a child from his grandfather about the head-hunting days. He wondered if it was a premeditated act by one of the tribesmen, considering that this was a tradition followed decades ago in these parts. He didn't want to assume anything. He wanted to collect as much information as possible, talk to witnesses, and take an account of things from the people present at the camp during the time of the murder. It was going to be a long night. But Angami was in no hurry. He had nothing and no one to return home to. Work was everything. So was solitude. For some reason, the inspector had a premonition that this was going to be a tough one to crack.

He sent two junior officers from his team to collect detailed information from the camp owner, David Konwang, and the guard, Bhansal, who had found the body. The crowd was getting boisterous, wanting to know what was happening. A few officers from the army had to be deployed to maintain order. A heartbreaking cry came from the outdoor balcony facing the tents. The inconsolable man was instantly surrounded by people trying to pacify him. Angami walked towards them.

'Who's that?' the inspector asked Ravinder, one of the officers.

'That's Aman Kumar. Tanya's boyfriend. Remember we saw a couple walk in a few days ago at Three Cheers Bar? Same one. Poor guy is a total mess, sir.'

No wonder Tanya had looked familiar. But with such a grotesque injury, he hadn't quite recognized her. Angami viewed the emotional outburst of the boyfriend with detachment. He had seen a lot of such theatrics in his time to be immediately swayed by any of them. As far as he was concerned, everyone at the camp, especially those who were close acquaintances of Tanya, was a suspect.

'Who would do this to her? Why Tanya? Why her?' The grieving man was hysterical.

Inspector Angami had never seen a grown man cry so much.

Could loss inflict such a deep wound? The inspector shrugged. What did he know of these things? His was an ordinary life. No grand love to remember, nor loss to grieve.

Perhaps the nature of his work made him the way he was. When you live on the dark side, something in you dies too. Love, trust, emotion, connections, bonding—all these become meaningless. Priorities change. Perhaps it was about building walls to keep out the constant demons he dealt with. And Angami knew the only way he could do that was to remain detached. Attachments made you weak. He had seen enough of life to know that it was at one's lowest point that walls crumbled, and the beast took residence. He made sure that that never happened to him. Loneliness, thus, was such sweet company. And no matter which part of the country he travelled to as part of the investigation team, a Leonard Cohen CD, a pack of Cuban cigars and a Glenfiddich bottle were all that was required to end the day. At forty-five years, he was a shadow of who he used to be. The unshaven, dishevelled look with the Bogart coat and hat had now become his signature style. His mind was as sharp as ever. Nothing missed his eye. Those who worked with him called him John Holmes. Inspector Angami had been involved in solving some of the most high-profile cases. The CBI often assigned him to the most dangerous, bizarre ones. It was his forte. He had come home to Kohima hoping for a restful two-week vacation. But that seemed like a distant possibility now.

'Please do this as a personal favour, John,' local MP Losou had requested. 'The Hornbill Festival is going on and we don't want this to affect the reputation of the show in any way. The relentless efforts of the government have just started to show results. Tourism is vital to our state, as you are aware.

It would mean a lot to us if you could solve this as soon and as quietly as possible.'

Angami was still observing Aman from a distance, focusing on his body language and expressions. The man was the prime suspect by default. He was crying with his face in his hands, looking up only when someone came over to comfort him. He was a good-looking chap, probably in his late thirties. Took good care of grooming himself, the inspector noted. The hair was perfect and the beard well-trimmed. The Hilfiger chino pants, the Mont Blanc shades in his shirt pocket, and the tattoos were also eye-catching. He could have easily passed for a model. Of course, Aman and Tanya had always looked like tourists. The locals could tell when it wasn't one of their own. Kohima was a small town. Everyone knew everyone else.

But tonight, Aman was an inconsolable man. He was flitting between hysterical crying and quiet sobbing. The inspector approached him. Talking to the closest kin of the victim was always difficult. It never got easy, no matter how many times you did it.

'Very sorry for your loss, Mr Kumar. I understand that this is difficult for you, but if it's okay with you, I would like to ask a few questions. It's our standard protocol. Could you tell me what happened? The sequence of events as clearly as you can remember, please.'

Aman tried to regain his composure before he spoke, tears still running down his face. 'We had quite a hectic day. Tanya and I were at the Myanmar border, at the refugee camp specifically, which had been torched down amid the recent violence. She was gathering a few eyewitness accounts. We got back by evening to attend the rock concert at the festival. The concert ended earlier than expected. 9.00 p.m. So, we came here for an early dinner before going to bed. We had a long trek ahead of us tomorrow—to Khonoma village. As soon as we reached the camp, which was around 9.30 p.m., she headed towards her tent to change. I went to the common washroom near the restaurant. I met Parashuram, the assistant chef at the restaurant, and spoke to him for a while regarding the menu. Tanya was in the mood for pasta. She loved Italian. I requested him to prepare that. It was then that we heard the security guard's screams. Nothing could prepare me for what I was going to see there.' He clasped Angami's hands and wept in them. 'Inspector, I cannot tell you what it feels like, you know. To have been there and not done a thing to save her.'

'I understand. Thank you. We will be in touch with you if we have more information regarding the murder. Right now, everything's premature. Also, if you remember any untoward incident that happened tonight, do call me,' said Angami as he handed Aman his card.

Aman nodded listlessly before drowning back in his private despair.

'Sid,' Angami said to one of his assistant officers, 'ask everyone who was at the camp from 9.00 p.m. to 10.30 p.m. to meet me here. We need to talk to them.'

He sat around the fire outside that had been prepared to keep the campers warm at night. Most of them hung around it for a drink or two while sharing the events of the day. Camp Kismar was the perfect place for tourists to network. But tonight, everyone was near the crime scene trying to get a sense of what had happened. The gory visuals were still fresh in Angami's mind. Not that he hadn't seen them before, but what did a woman as fearless and beautiful as Tanya do to deserve a fate as horrific as this?

The inspector knew that time would reveal all. He dreaded being the vessel that carried everyone's darkest truths. But investigations often unearthed many skeletons. In the days and weeks to come, he knew there would be a lot he would have to confront. He had lived in the 'abyss', as he called it, for far too long. For decades, he had spent day after day chasing murderers, sociopaths, psychopaths, paedophiles, sex offenders, etc. Once, he was even stabbed in the chest and another time, shot in the leg. All that had taken its toll. The loneliness, insomnia, inability to emote or feel deeply, addiction to tobacco and alcohol… They were occupational hazards, Angami often said. He wondered where the bohemian idealistic youth of his adolescence had disappeared. At forty-five, he felt eighty years old.

Officer Siddharth came back with four men in tow.

'I demand to know what's going on. I had finally gone back to sleep after all the fiasco outside when this guy rudely woke me up.'

John Angami studied the agitated man. He looked kind of important. Or he seemed to think he was.

'Sorry to disturb you at this time of night, sir. But considering there has been a murder within the camp premises, this was inevitable.'

'I know that. But why am I here?'

'Your presence here at the time of the crime is why you have been summoned, sir. The five of you were near the crime scene when the murder happened, and I just wanted to verify your account and make a crime scene log.'

'Are you telling me that I am a suspect?' the man fumed.

'Mr Ram Prasad Nair, an MP from Kerala, right? I am sorry to have interrupted your vacation, sir. But we have procedures to follow. Could you recount your whereabouts concisely so that we can relieve you sooner?' Angami's tone was rising. Politicians always had that effect on him due to their sense of entitlement. He tried to regain his composure.

'Inspector John Angami, that's your name, isn't it?' said the man condescendingly, looking at his nametag. 'All it takes is one phone call to stop this midnight interrogation. I am sure you are aware of that.'

The inspector had become so accustomed to such high-handedness that he wasn't flustered by the minister's threats.

'I am very aware, sir. But I also hope you are aware that this is a homicide investigation. An FIR will be registered and will place the five of you, including the guard, at the scene of the crime. I have no other option than to hear out each of your versions. But if you want to complicate things for yourself, you are free to do so.'

The minister huffed and puffed. Angami laughed inwardly at the man's inflated ego.

'I was in a meeting all day with members of the Democratic Alliance. You can verify the same with Mr Dieke Losou, your MLA. We began the session around 10.30 a.m. and it went on until 8.00 p.m. After dinner, Mr Losou dropped me back at the camp. I then retired to my tent.'

'So, this was around?'

'Approximately 9.45 p.m.' The minister was visibly irritated.

'And in that time, you did not see or hear anything unusual, did you, sir?'

'No, I did not. Like I said, I was too tired.'

'Isn't it strange that when the screams of the security guard shook up the entire camp, you were fast asleep?' Angami said.

'What can I say? I am a deep sleeper,' Ram Nair replied sarcastically.

'Ah, okay. Nice alibi, sir. You can leave now if you wish.'

'You are trying to intimidate me, Inspector. I am telling you the truth, but you are calling it an alibi?'

Angami didn't bother to look up, as he was busy writing in the logbook. The minister paced along the walkway to the campfire, frantically trying to call someone on his phone.

'Must be trying to contact his *chamcha* friends in the bureau,' Ravi commented, laughing out loud.

'Let him. He's just wasting his time,' Angami remarked in irritation.

'Sir, Mr Nicholas Kent is here, the Danish tourist.'

Mr Kent was an aristocratic-looking gentleman. A Caucasian, he was probably in his late thirties or early forties. He sat next to the inspector. The fire was weakening, and the chill of the night was seeping into everyone's bones. There was a belief amongst some of the local tribes that when someone was brutally murdered, the spirits of their ancestors gathered around the body in order to placate it and drive away its misery. It was close to midnight now and everyone was on edge. Until the crime log had been filled in and an FIR registered, Angami was in no mood to wrap up for the night. Siddharth and Ravinder groaned inwardly.

Nicolas Kent handed over his documents, including his visa and passport, for inspection.

'Tell me the purpose of your visit, Mr Kent, and the events that led to your presence here.'

'I am with National Geographic, sir.' He showed Angami his ID.

'I came here to cover the Hornbill Festival. I have been doing this for the past several years. NG has a special feature edition on it. I have been a regular visitor to Kohima for some time—around seven to eight years, to be exact—as part of a project on the Konyak Nagas, the last head-hunters of Nagaland. So, Kohima is like my second home. I met Tanya in one of the local bars several years back. The last time she was here, she was busy with her ongoing project concerning the Rohingyas. I told her I wanted to cover the story. She agreed and this morning, we both travelled to the refugee camp at the Myanmar border along with her friend Aman. The three of us returned by 7.30 p.m. Aman and Tanya went for the concert, while I was at the camp looking through the photographs we took earlier today and uploading them to the hard disk. I then showered and headed off for the woods close by, hoping to get a few shots of the area at night. The moon is spectacular tonight if you've noticed.'

Angami looked at the sky. Indeed it was. This supermoon was the largest he had ever seen.

'This supermoon is a beauty,' continued Kent. 'But according to pagan legends, it is also the night of the evil's resurrection. As Hippocrates once said, one who is seized with terror, fright and madness during the night is being visited by the goddess of the moon. Do you remember that?'

Angami shuddered at the description. If only the skies and trees and all that bore witness to the night could talk. The murderer was inside the camp this very minute, perhaps watching everything unfold before him.

'Go on, Mr Kent. What happened after that?'

'I got a couple of splendid shots of the moon and returned to the camp for dinner probably around 10.00 p.m. Mr Kabir joined me at the table. We chatted a bit and then I retired to my tent. That's when I heard the screams. I rushed out to see what had happened. By then, a large crowd was gathering near the camp and there was a lot of confusion. Within a few minutes, I saw you guys arrive. I was part of the crowd.'

'Did you notice anything unusual at the camp tonight? Anything that might have caught your attention?'

'I can't recall anything specific.'

'Thank you, Mr Kent. We will be in touch with you if we need further information.' Angami paused, looking at him for a while. 'You seem to have hurt yourself, Mr Kent. There are a few bruises on your left elbow.'

'Oh, yes, brushed past a branch in the forest. Need to attend to this. Goodnight, everyone,' Kent said before walking away.

Angami took out a cigarette. He could sense a headache was coming on.

'Kabir Wasim,' Officer Ravinder called out, summoning the next witness. The fire was dying out and it was getting terribly cold. 'Couldn't he have conducted this inside?' Ravi murmured irritably to his colleague.

Everyone turned to look around. The Bollywood actor walked in. He was a tall, stunningly good-looking man. His chiselled facial features were partially hidden by his thick, exquisite beard. There was no mistaking this man's swag genes. His eyes were kind of grey, almost silver-grey. At first glance, he could easily be mistaken for someone from the Middle East. There was something about him that moved you. His face was forlorn.

'Kabir Wasim here. Hi.' The actor shook hands with Angami.

'Sorry to question you guys at such an odd hour. But this is just the standard procedure.'

'That's okay, Inspector. I wasn't getting much sleep anyway. Do you mind if I light a cigarette?'

'No problem at all. Please tell us where you were this evening, Mr Kabir.'

The actor took a long drag. He appeared to have jumped right out of a movie frame. 'I came to Kohima last evening. From Mumbai actually, where I had recently met with a small accident,' he said, pointing towards his fractured elbow. 'I took some time off from work and came here to relax. A group of us went to Shilloi Lake this morning for a bit of trekking and fishing and got back by evening. Around 7.00 p.m., I went to the concert at the festival and returned to the camp by 8.30 p.m. I met Tanya on the way, and we talked for a bit. It's hard to believe she's no more…' Kabir had a faraway look on his face. Angami noticed his eyes were tearing up, but the actor regained his composure instantly. 'After dinner, I went back to my tent and was reading when I heard the screams. I thought nothing of it, presuming it was probably drunk college kids getting boisterous at night while returning from the Hornbill venue. It was only when I heard the police siren and commotion outside that I went out and got to know what had happened.'

'Your tent is just a few feet away from Tanya's, right? Did you hear any unusual movement or struggle of any sort at the time?'

'Inspector, if I had, I assure you I would not have ignored it. I would have broken the bastard's hand!' Kabir was losing his cool and could barely talk. He took a deep breath to calm himself. 'I had my earphones on and was listening to music. So, I heard nothing. Yes, I am in Tent #10 and Tanya was in #14—' His voice wavered, and he looked away, as if he couldn't talk anymore.

'Did you both know each other before?' Angami studied him very closely.

Kabir hesitated. He paused for a while before answering. 'No, we didn't. I met her here.'

'Right then. Thank you, Mr Wasim. We will be in touch with you.'

The actor looked quite frazzled. It was obvious that the murder had affected him more than he cared to admit. Not much was known about Kabir Wasim's life except that he came from a very middle-class background, having grown up in Gujarat. And that he had to struggle a lot to get where he was now. He kept his personal life very private.

What lies in the hearts of men is not easily knowable, Angami pondered as he watched Kabir leave. Who knows what dark secrets each of us carry within. We wear masks to hide our inherent masks as part of social conditioning. Masks are there for conformity. They are as necessary as armour. Society has a structure. And it is essential to act out our lives within that structure. We all eventually forget who we truly are, Angami said to himself.

He snapped out of his introspection and surveyed everyone around him. He wished he could read their minds like a mentalist. 'Sonder.' That is exactly what Angami wished he could do right now. Read their stories. All five of them. That way, he could wrap up the case much sooner.

David Konwang was to be interrogated next. He was the owner of Camp Kismar: a proud Konyak youth, his entrepreneurial skills had earned him a badge of honour from the Nagaland Tourism department. He was singularly responsible for showcasing Naga heritage to the world. Camp Kismar was his pet project and everything about the Hornbill Festival revolved around the camp. At twenty-nine years, he was the youngest Naga to hold the honour of being the cultural ambassador of the state. Angami had known him for years as a quiet child growing up at the local orphanage. It was very inspiring to see how successful David had become.

'Inspector, this is so damaging to the reputation of Camp Kismar. Never has such an incident, let alone one as horrendous as this one, ever happened.'

David was deeply disturbed. The inspector could guess how Tanya's murder was going to impact his business in a major way. Tourists were superstitious about such events.

'I knew her well, you know. She had been a regular here for the past five years. She helped us a lot during our media campaigns for the Hornbill Festival and Camp Kismar. We were recently part of an effort to provide shelter and hideout to a few Rohingya refugees. After the recent clashes, most of their homes were burnt down. She was such a humane person. She loved everyone as her own. And most of us who knew her adored her. An amazing, inspiring woman. I can't imagine who would do such a thing. And such a brutal crime. Yeah, sure, she had taken on some big names with the recent exposé, but even then.' David had started talking even before Angami posed any questions.

The inspector sensed a powerful energy around Tanya. Even in death, she radiated that aura. The effect she had on people around her was testimony to this fact.

'There was a crime waiting to happen, I guess, though one never thought it would be murder. She made a lot of enemies along the way. There were a lot of far-right folks here too, in Kohima, who were disillusioned with her aggressive approach to changing the refugee policy. I often disagreed with her on many things. Things she never understood about our culture and the Naga way of life.'

David's face looked expressionless for a moment. There seemed to be some sort of confusion in his mind, and he was lost in his own thoughts.

'Where were you around the time of the murder, David?'

David snapped out of his ruminations. 'I was at the concert venue with a few of my biker campers. We were planning to later hang out at the pub for drinks and dinner. Tanya and Aman were also with us before they changed their minds and headed towards the camp upon calling it a night. An hour later, Mahesh, my manager at the camp, rings me up and tells me there's been an incident. By the time we reached the camp, everything was over. We couldn't even go near her tent. The scene of the crime was secured. All I could see was Tanya lying there—her eyes wide open and her blood still fresh, trickling on to the ground. It looked so surreal. I could not hold myself together and broke down. For God's sake, we had just spoken to her 15 minutes back, man.' David couldn't talk further.

'I assure you this investigation will move forward with the utmost speed. Will let you know if we need any further help.'

David thanked Angami and walked back towards the camp. Suri, David's assistant, met him near the camp lobby. It seemed as if they had broken into a heated discussion. Suri's hands were flying all over the place. He seemed very agitated. The lad was autistic, Angami was informed. David was trying to pacify him and take him to the staff quarters.

The inspector had known David since childhood. They belonged to the same Baptist church. Not that Angami was religious, but he too was a creature of habit. After all, faith gives people a sense of belonging and hope when nothing else does. David was an orphan who had grown up at the orphanage run by the church. He had an uncle, a distant relative, who was a tribal chieftain and a very famous head-hunter in his day. He used to stay with his uncle occasionally. David's parents had died in a bus accident when he was just two years old. He had no immediate relatives except for the distant uncle, an old man in his seventies at the time. So the church adopted him. Incidentally, it was the same church where Angami too grew up.

Tonight, Angami felt proud seeing how David had emerged as a successful young entrepreneur. Yet there was something about him that was amiss. Angami sighed. It had been a long night and there were still two more witnesses to interview.

The camp was deserted by the time it was all over. The crowd had left and the only people still scavenging through the crime scene were the forensic experts and a few officers from the crime branch. Angami noticed a familiar face there.

'Dr Laxmi, it's Inspector Angami here.'

'Hello, Inspector. I have heard a lot about you.'

Dr Laxmi was one of the finest forensic experts at the bureau. John remembered seeing her last at one of the crime scenes where he was investigating a couple of years ago. She was an intern then. It surprised him that the government had got directly involved in his latest case and actually sent someone from the CBI's forensic team. He wondered why there was so much interest from the government in solving the case. Was it due to Mr Nair, considering the minister was already embroiled in an ongoing trafficking scandal and wanted to protect his name at all costs? Or was it Mr Losou, the Naga minister who would do anything to salvage the festival's reputation? Or perhaps it was so because Tanya had already become a UN ambassador of sorts with her work. This could snowball into an international scandal, as the minister had mentioned.

It could embarrass the government pretty badly.

'What do we have so far, Doctor?'

'We have collected the swabs and blood samples, sir. We are now scouring the area for any shreds of fabric or other elements inadvertently left behind by the killer.'

'What are your first impressions, Doctor?'

'Can't say, Inspector. The crime is an extremely violent one. The incision in the neck looks like the work of an expert. Probably used a kitchen knife or a *dao*, a thick double-edged, corrugated antique sword-knife that the Konyak head-hunters used back in the day. He was probably determined at first but lost steam midway, leaving the cut half-done and an inch short of damaging the tracheal tube. There are fingerprints around her neck and wrists, suggesting a possible struggle. The attacker may have first tried to strangle her. In fact it's certain that he did that first, got her unconscious and then tried to decapitate. Also, there is a possibility that there were two people involved. The first person could have assisted in restraining her while the second killed her. We can't rule this out either.'

Dr Laxmi was now standing behind Angami, enacting the crime. 'The killer stood behind her to decapitate. It would have been difficult to stand in front of the victim or place her in a kneeling position for decapitation in a space as small as this tent. His accomplice must have been holding her to maintain her posture. By the manner of the incision on the right side of the neck, the killer was definitely left-handed.'

'Does it seem to be the work of a Konyak head-hunter, Doctor?'

'I thought of that as well. But it seems unlikely, as the practice has long been extinct. And the head-hunters of those days are all octogenarians now. They're too weak to kill or have a motive. There was a lot of rage in whoever did this. It could be a revenge killing, a crime of passion or, heaven forbid, a psychopathic killer's handiwork. But it was definitely a copycat killing, inspired by the head-hunting tradition. These are my initial assumptions. Have you retrieved the murder weapon, Inspector, or is it missing?'

'It's missing. The killer probably took it with him or hid it elsewhere. We checked the entire perimeter when we arrived.'

'I hope the crime scene wasn't contaminated. We face the burden of such errors in most investigations.'

'I doubt that, Doctor. The security guard, Bhansal, was the main witness and then Aman, the victim's boyfriend. These two were at the scene of the crime when I arrived. No one else. Tanya, however, was in Aman's arms.'

'That is enough for the murderer's fingerprint to be erased or any fabric or hair to have transferred onto Aman's person and those of Aman to have lodged onto the victim. Which could possibly incriminate him as the main suspect. I am sure you are aware of that.'

What Dr Laxmi was saying was true. Years of being on the field had taught Angami how securing the crime scene was one of the most crucial tasks in a successful investigation. But that was next to impossible because someone or the other always reached before the responders did. Most often, the relatives themselves, overwhelmed and unable to contain their emotions, smeared the victim's blood onto themselves or some such by holding or embracing them in moments of shock or sadness.

'True, Doctor. But compared to what we usually see, we took over pretty early on in this case. I am certain that any contamination would be minimal. Let's take Aman's clothes too for the forensic evaluation. I will let him know. We need every tiny bit we can get.'

Aman's blue sweater and jeans were soaked in blood. He collected the clothes and handed them over to the forensic team.

After making sure that every inch of the crime scene had been thoroughly checked, the body taken to the forensic morgue for the post-mortem, and all possible witnesses questioned, Angami told his team to retire for the night while he went back to the station HQ about a mile away from Camp Kismar. The FIR was to be filed in court the very next day.

After a while, he went over the document while making a mental note of things.

Time of death: Definitely around 10.00 p.m., considering all the witnesses' accounts.

Cause of death: Strangulation and partial decapitation; injuries on the arms, shoulders and neck, possibly due to a struggle, to be confirmed after the post-mortem.

Murder weapon: A knife. Possibly a kitchen knife or a chopper or a dao.

Main witnesses: Aman and Bhansal.

Secondary witnesses: The politician Ram Prasad Nair, the photographer Nicholas Kent, the famous actor Kabir Wasim, and the tour guide (and probably a Konyak Naga) David Konwang.

One victim, five main suspects and no possible motives so far. Angami knew that he would have to dig much deeper into the victim's and the witnesses' stories before even coming to any semblance of a conclusion. And then there was the task of retrieving the missing murder weapon. For all he knew, it could be flung somewhere into the impenetrable valleys of the Japfu range by now. He thought about the conversation he had had with all of them, looking for cues or micro-expressions. Something that would give them away. Something that he could build on. It was 3.30 a.m. Sleep was slowly overpowering him. Angami closed the files and locked the cabinet. The chilly wintry night hurt his eyes when he stepped out. A lone wolf was howling somewhere. The moon was still gloriously large and silver. *Supermoon, the night of the evil's resurrection.* Kent's words echoed in his mind as he reached home and drifted to sleep.

2

The thing about Indian police headquarters, especially in small towns, is that they follow a façade prototype. Kohima Central was no different. The dilapidated walls, chandelier-like cobwebs, dusty furniture, tonnes and tonnes of files stacked haphazardly in no particular order, et al. How investigators scoured through it all was still a mystery. Computers still hadn't made their way into the Kohima police station. And khaki was still the colour of their uniform. Not a flattering one, especially against such an uninspiring backdrop. The uniform actually made things look worse.

Angami, however, loved his job. A graduate of the Sardar Vallabhbhai Patel Police Academy, John Angami was always at the top of his class. He had a nose for problem-solving, his professors used to say. After graduation, Angami's first posting, in the summer of '92, was in Merapani, a 400 km stretch encompassing a border village which was the hotbed of the conflict between Assam and Nagaland. When Nagaland was formed in 1963, its borders were clearly defined on paper, but on the ground, little was done. Tensions between Nagaland and Assam arose at this time. There were armed clashes between the police forces and the people. The carnage of 1985 was still on everyone's mind. It took a long time for Angami to gain their trust. His main task was to convince the villagers that he was not there to support the intermediaries on either side but to make sure that peace prevailed in the village for the people to move on with their lives. The interstate border conflict had taken an economic toll. He convinced them that he genuinely cared about their plight and wanted to make a difference. Slowly, with time, he gained their trust and respect. The villagers came to him with their problems, and almost always, he found a way.

The villagers loved him because unlike other officers before him, he was genuinely trying to make a difference in their lives. Most often, he played the interlocutor between the villagers and the state government. This was a watershed moment in his career, facilitating lasting peace in the region between the Nagas and the Assamese. He became instrumental when peace talks were initiated by the central government for the two factions in Dimapur. And from then on, it was one roller-coaster ride of a career.

Angami sipped his morning coffee as he filed the FIR. Officer Siddharth would deliver it to the district court to help the investigation move ahead. Angami was in a nostalgic mood. He thought of the losses that he had suffered in his career. Of his aides, sources, trust—sometimes, even his soul. He felt tired. Forty-five was too young to retire. Yet the dark side had taken its toll. God knows the inspector had enough of his own demons to fight. Years of being exposed to such violent crimes and criminals had desensitized him in several ways. He had no family to call his own. His mother had died at the hands of a drunk, violent man—his father—when Angami was just five years old. Faces and images encountered during the day haunted his dreams at night. Many times, their voices persisted in his head, as did the smell of death. There was no telling what the long-term effects of such work were on officers like him. Such was the nature of the beast he had to contend with daily.

For now, there was a lot of work to be completed. As soon as the judge took cognisance of the FIR, full-fledged investigations could begin. The sun was bright and scorching outside. It would be a few hours before the chill of the night seeped in again. Angami wanted to bask in its warmth for a while. Little things like this gave him solace.

The autopsy reports came in after a few days. As predicted, the primary cause of death was strangulation and secondary, mutilation. There were all kinds of stories doing the rounds. The local news media had a blast covering the crime. But Angami had other views as well. One would think the killer was an original head-hunter belonging to the Konyaks or a copycat one. But there were other possibilities too which couldn't be negated. In this particular case of homicide, personal, professional and even political vendettas couldn't be ruled out. One thing was for sure. The criminal was an expert. To have suffocated an adult woman without a sound being heard outside and then partially decapitated her, all in a matter of 10 to 15 minutes, required a certain level of expertise. There were two people involved for sure. And the rage. He could not fathom the rage that directed the perpetrator to commit such heinousness.

Angami kept looking at Tanya's pictures. Even in death, her face had an indefinable grace. There was an aura about her despite what had been done to her. He wondered if her soul was watching from elsewhere. The Nagas believed that after death, the spirit lingered near the body, mourning for days. The spirit was everything in tribal faith. It was endless, eternal. The body died and decayed, but the spirit always found another vessel to continue its journey forward depending on its karma.

The tribes in Nagaland had deep reverence for spirits. Their entire culture revolved around them. The inspector's tribe, the Angamis, believed in the afterlife. Good souls went to live with the sky god, whereas the sinners had to spend seven lives on earth. Some of those who could not reach the sky god were cursed to wander as spirits on earth. The inspector wondered which dimension Tanya Singh would occupy.

Both Ravinder and Siddharth, the junior officers, were told to bring in detailed background information about the victim within a few days. They were running out of time. Already a week had passed. This had to be wrapped up soon or it could create a political fallout in Kohima. Tanya's phone records showed around seven calls made to Aman and some to two unknown numbers. Their caller IDs weren't listed. On further questioning, Aman Kumar revealed that one of the numbers belonged to her old school friend Zahira Choudhary, who was a journalist based in Delhi. Zahira and Tanya used to work together at the *Sunday Mail* until Tanya shifted base to Mumbai for the *India Times*. Angami called Zahira, introduced himself and informed her of Tanya's death. There was silence on the other end and then quiet sobbing. He asked if he could see her in the evening. She agreed. There was an Air India flight at noon every day, from Dimapur to Delhi. He would be able to reach there on time.

'Did Tanya ever receive any threats?' Angami asked Aman.

'All the time. She was trolled big time on social media. We had to approach the cyber cell several times to lodge complaints. Once, someone was outside her apartment, stalking her for a week. Especially with the latest exposé on sex trafficking among the top brass in the political establishment, death threats had become a regular affair. She never took them that seriously. Most journalists in the country today are at the receiving end of such things. One of the accused, incidentally, is right here in Kohima.'

'That I am aware of, Aman. Ram Nair? I also came to know very recently that you work for him.' Angami studied Aman's reaction closely.

Aman looked surprised. Perhaps because his connection with Ram Nair was quite classified. He was probably an undercover resource for the minister's dubious network, Angami speculated.

'I did work for him. Not anymore.'

'Why is that?'

'He wanted me to spy on Tanya using my personal connection with her and retrieve a vital piece of evidence. A pendrive with all the material proof. He even suggested that I intimidate her. I refused and threatened him that if he so much as even touched her, he'd be answerable to me.'

'I see.'

'She became very unpopular after her special feature on the Rohingya crisis and the government's apathetic attitude towards the refugees. Her involvement with the UNHCR gave her the leeway to put international pressure on the government to be a signatory to the UN Refugee Convention. There was, however, a concerted political campaign against her efforts. Especially after the drugs and sex trafficking exposé which involved young Rohingya girls. She received threats online and offline.' Aman had a faraway look in his eyes. 'But Tanu never gave a shit. That's how she was. So freaking fearless.' His voice cracked, giving way to his emotions.

'She sounds like a remarkable woman,' said Angami, sighing.

'She was. I needed her strength more than she needed my love. We had broken up, but I couldn't imagine a life without her in it. It was a kind of symbiotic relationship, hers and mine.'

'The day of the murder, you were at the Myanmar border refugee camp. Did you notice anything out of the ordinary, Aman?'

'No. Not at all. Maybe a slight altercation Tanya had with the border patrol when one of them was manhandling a Rohingya woman. Tanya was visibly agitated, and I had to intervene to calm her down. The soldier looked irked but restrained himself. She spent some more time talking to the women at the camp before a few BSF personnel came and asked us to leave. Tanya showed them her ID, but they wouldn't hear of it. "Security risk," they said. She was quite upset. It was her last day, and she wanted to meet more refugee eyewitnesses before she left.'

'Any idea what this story was about?'

'She was looking into the recent riot that had broken out at the refugee camp. She had one main witness, Mohsina Khan. She was gathering information and documenting data to convince the government to see the utter inhumanity of their decision to send the refugees back to Myanmar. She felt the move was politically pre-orchestrated. She wanted to report about that.'

'This project she was working on…do you have those files with you?'

Aman hesitated.

'Trust me, this will be confidential,' Angami assured him. 'She told me something in confidence two nights ago. If,

God forbid, anything happened to her, I was to get these files to Zahira and Kabir. It was as though she had a premonition. The pendrive has dozens of videos, audio interviews and voice notes prepared by Tanya. This is the evidence Ram Nair was also after. These contain stories within stories.' Aman handed the pendrive to Angami.

'I will be meeting Zahira tonight. But before that, I need to go through this.'

'Sure, Inspector. Do I need to stay here until the investigations are over? Tanya's parents are coming over today. In all probability, the funeral will be held in Kohima itself. She loved this place as her own. Called it her *soul place*.'

'I am afraid you and the other witnesses will need to be around until we finish the preliminary investigations, Aman. At least a week more.'

'I am okay with that. I need closure. It's as if she never left.'

The anatomy of loss—who among us can quantify it? Angami was lost in his thoughts. He had lived his life carrying the burden of such losses. Of all human woes, nothing was more tragic or impactful. The thing about death is that it weaves its own web of unpredictability with such precision that those of us left behind are left unaware, unable to cope with the fatality of things to come. That black hole in our hearts and minds that we are left to fill for the rest of our lives. All we can do is accept the inescapability of our own fragmented reality and memory. Such is life. A balance sheet of gains and losses.

Aman looked haggard, as if he hadn't slept in days. His eyes were dark and sunken. Angami felt sorry for him. He looked broken. He couldn't help but notice the tattoos on his arm. There was an intricate mandala tattoo on one hand, and on the other, there was a portrait of a mermaid. The face was so unique, like that of a goddess. The inspector wondered who it was. He had this inexplicable quality of being able to read people. Observing even the smallest detail about them and figuring things out. In fact, he had even done a course in micro-expression training and behavioural analysis. It helped having those skills. Over time, that translated into a powerful ESP.

The lady at the check-in counter was kind enough to upgrade Angami's seat to business class. It would be a three-hour flight, and he was hoping to go through the files on the pendrive that Aman had given him. He had no idea how much data was in there but wanted to peruse it all before he gave it to Ms Choudhary. Thankfully, there was no one else seated next to him. When he opened the pendrive, he found a lot of folders on it. At least 50. He didn't quite know where to start. 'Birthday', 'Journal', 'Blog', 'Banking', 'Articles', 'Login', 'Rohingya', etc.

He opened the first file which was named Rohingya. It was the documentary Tanya had been working on.

There were hundreds of pictures, a few videos and some journal entries that seemed like transcripts of the video. It was Mohsina's narrative and Tanya was the interviewer. The video was grainy. Probably taken with a phone camera to avoid the suspicion of the guards at the camp. Angami opened the transcript journal. It had several parts. This was going to be a long read, he thought to himself.

◆

Transcript #1

Tanya Singh: Through this documentary, I have tried to collect relevant information to summarize the Rohingya crisis the best way I could. There are children, women and men who have not just been driven out of their homeland but also faced unbelievable horrors in their home countries as well as within the countries they later fled to. Rape, murder, human trafficking, etc., have become a way of life for them. In a series of interviews with Mohsina Khan, a spokesperson at the Rohingya refugee crisis centre at the Rohingya camp in Kohima, the trials undergone by the Rohingyas, 'the forgotten people without an identity', are revealed. This is her story.

Mohsina: My name is Mohsina Khan. I am twenty-four years old. I am a Rohingya Muslim from the state of Rakhine, Myanmar.

We belong to a community of labourers and farmers from Myanmar. Our ancestors originally belonged to Bangladesh. They were employed by the state of Rangoon as building labourers when the city started developing under British rule. My family travelled from Dhaka to Rangoon in 1920. My great-grandfather, Hisham Khan, believed that his fortunes would increase greatly in Burma (as it was called during the colonial era). He went there as a labourer and in a few years' time, he started his own business as a street food vendor. He began doing very well and opened a chain of outlets which were later upgraded to full-fledged restaurants. He was living his dream and creating a legacy of his own in Rangoon.

In his mind, Burma was his home now. He could not think of any other. He fell in love with my great-grandmother, who was a Buddhist Burmese. They got married and my great-grandmother of course converted. By the time their two sons grew up, British rule ended with the culmination of World War II. The Battle of Rangoon had taken its toll on

Burma. Even under British rule, the Bamar community of the indigenous locals was growing restless with the large number of Indian labourers who were being brought in from the Indian subcontinent. They saw these new entrants as responsible for the erosion of their traditional culture and for the loss of job opportunities.

When the Japanese invaded, the Bamars readily joined hands with them against the British. They formed the Burma Independence Army. The BIA was instrumental in getting Burmese independence from the British with the help of the Japanese. After the bombing of Rangoon in 1941, the Japanese took over the country and the Allied forces retreated, creating chaos. There was a mass exodus, with a large Indian population and those of mixed origin (Indo-Burmese, Anglo-Indian, Anglo-Burmese) fleeing Burma, fearing the Japanese as well as the hostile native Bamars. During World War II, the Bamars allied with the Japanese and the ethnic minorities were on the side of the British. Thus began intense suspicion and conflict between the two. My grandfather would recount those horrific days. He was only eight then. The restaurants were destroyed in the bombing, and the vendor carriages confiscated and looted. The family had nothing in their hands except the clothes that they wore and a sum equivalent to INR 10,000 that my great-grandfather carefully sewed into the coat he was wearing.

There was no telling what could happen. There was anarchy everywhere. People were being killed in the streets. My great-grandfather put his wife and sons on a boat and came to the Arakan islands in the state of Rakhine. He still believed in the idea of Burma. While many of our neighbours and friends sought refuge in other countries, he refused to go anywhere else. But the Burmese Army had reached the Rakhine province and instigated a Buddhist and Muslim riot. It was their agenda to cleanse Burma of 'foreign intruders and incursion'. That was the beginning of the many horrors that we, the Rohingyas, had to face as the single-most persecuted people in the history of mankind. Hisham Khan had no idea of the grave repercussions of the choices he made. And generations of our people have had to pay the price for it.

Tanya: By 1948, a new government was in place. Mohsina's great-grandfather had to work in rice fields. Life wasn't easy. They were not given citizenship. They were denied basic rights and were constantly discriminated against and denigrated. Mohsina's grandfather recounted the time when during the 1960s young Rohingyas who couldn't take the humiliation anymore registered themselves with the Rohingya Mujahideen, an insurgent group. Many resistance attacks were coordinated across Burma, killing several civilians. The government launched massive military operations against the insurgent groups. Her grandfather's brother, Iqbal Khan, was killed in one such operation. He was a member of the RM.

Mohsina: On a quiet April day in 1978, Operation King Dragon was on as the military searched every house on the streets of Rakhine, targeting suspected Mujahideens and shot them point blank in broad daylight. Iqbal Khan was one of them. My great-grandfather died of heartbreak soon after. He could not live with the fact that he had outlived his son. He blamed himself for all the misfortunes that plagued our family. 'If only I had left for Calcutta like the others.' You see, such is the scourge of an ethnic conflict. The Union of Burma refused to recognize us as its legal citizens because we had no documentary proof of our residence in Rangoon before

1948. Governments came and went. My grandfather and father were still farmers, struggling to support their families and trying to give us a good education and protect our identity as Rohingyas, the citizens of the Union of Burma. But what do you do when the very state that you feel allegiance to disowns you? Generations of our people suffered and still do. This is our story. Hopefully, someone someday will watch this and save us from our existential purgatory. Thank you, Tanya Didi, for giving us this opportunity.

◆

Transcript #2

Tanya: In some regions of the world such as Rakhine, the gloom persisted as if it was eternal. And in those places, the darkest acts of humanity thrived. There was no conscience. No moral fibre to keep in check the body counts that fell as twilight came. Here, the dark wolves howled at the moon each night. While faceless men with muted identities were buried in mass graves, no one talked of them or went in search of them. There was no time to mourn. Or count their losses. Their tears dried and hearts grew cold. Life went on, with or without their loved ones. It was always a struggle for survival.

Mohsina: My father, Ahmed Khan, was not very happy when I was born. Still reeling under the bane of financial difficulties bordering on poverty, he was trying hard to make ends meet. I was the youngest of three girls. Mehr and Zoya, my older sisters, are twins and two years older than me. My father worried about how he would marry off his daughters. And in those days, girls were liabilities. Crimes against women were rampant. The army's atrocities were well-known. Normal folks were caught between the avenging Mujahideen and the rage of the Buddhist monks and the army. My father argued that men could defend themselves. Put up a fight and die if need be. But when you had daughters instead of sons, every minute of every hour was spent worrying about their safety. He never showed his disappointment towards us. And yet his anxiety every time there were raids or random checks, was obvious.

We lived in a thatched-roof hut by the coast in the capital city of Sittwe, an estuarial island created by the confluence of the Kaladan, Mayu and Lay Mro rivers that flowed into the Bay of Bengal. Rakhine, despite its turmoil, is a beautiful region on the west coast of Myanmar. The lush-green paddy fields and coconut trees, the Bay of Bengal, and the Arakan mountains around it could have made Rakhine a dream destination. It could have been one of the most prosperous regions in Burma if not for the ethnic conflict that held the majority of us economic hostage for decades. Magnificent pagodas were strewn across its rural landscape. They stood as testimony to the Buddhist culture that was deeply rooted in the Burmese state.

Governments came and went, democratic as well as military. But nothing changed for us. We were still the stateless Bengalis. Our politicians took offence when anyone called us Rohingyas. To them, we were always Bengalis. We don't look like the Burmese, or act like them, nor pray like them. But this had always been our land…what we called home. Our history can be traced back to the eighth century, yet Myanmar's law does not recognize us. We are restricted from accessing education, healthcare and job opportunities.

We were the dispensable outliers. We were branded as terrorists and the scum of the universe. If there are any people who have been denigrated consistently by the collective world, it is us. When you don't have an identity, what do you call yourself? What did the Jews call themselves in Germany? Germans? They were relocated to Israel after they paid a heavy price. It helped them rebuild their lives and continue their bloodline. Will we ever have such a place to call our own? Or are we doomed to become extinct, persecuted until the last man standing falls by the grazing bullet?

My sisters and I, we found a refuge in the security and love that our parents tried to provide us. We ran across the fields catching butterflies and frogs. We played in puddles and laughed until our bellies hurt. We never went beyond the village boundary. The soldiers will take you away, they warned us. We were like an island in ourselves. Ammi and Abba made sure we had food to eat and never went hungry despite our condition. If the harvest season did not do well, Abba went with the fishermen to the Bay and sold fish in the market. When I think back, the thing that upsets me most is how Abba struggled to keep us alive, yet the local police were always troubling him on some pretext or the other. Some days, it would be for ID proof, and on other days, it would be for his licence to sell his produce. When they could not get to the insurgents, they would turn their anger on the local Rohingyas. They liked Abba though, as he was an honest man. He respected the law and did everything to keep away from reactionary groups.

Mehr, Zoya and I went to a local school nearby. I had made up my mind at the age of seven that I wanted to help my family out of our existential crisis, and the only way I could do that was by having an education. I wanted to be a journalist. The head teacher at my school was a kind woman,

Mrs Noor Faizal. There were only two teachers at school. And we were 35 students. Mrs Noor was everyone's favourite. She was a petite woman who inspired us each day with her oratory and narrative skills. She would recount stories of the world outside Myanmar.

'Once you have an education and a job and make enough money, you need to travel the world or perhaps settle in another country where freedom, justice and liberty are a given. Where human rights and empathy were a way of life, rather than the oppression of the weak. We don't have to live like this forever. We can take destiny into our hands and rewrite our stories,' Mrs Noor said. She always had our rapt attention. When we would go back home and tell Abba and Ammi these stories, Abba would laugh at them and say that our teacher was too idealistic and that she shouldn't fill our heads with unrealistic dreams. But in my heart, I knew that we would someday fulfil these aspirations.

3

Transcript #3

Mohsina: 2012 was a year when everything changed. It was also a year that made zombies out of men. Maybe every Rohingya generation was destined to witness the terror of their existential despair. We were constantly fed the affirmation that this was the will of God. But for me, that year, God died. And in his place was born the resilient faith in myself. That was the only thing that was going to keep us alive. The only thing that was persistent in our minds: the will to survive.

We were returning from school that evening. I was discussing with Zoya and Mehr about Mrs Noor's assignment. I love her assignments, I told them. They helped me think very differently. We were talking animatedly about it when from afar, we saw smoke rising. Perhaps they are flattening the land again to grow crops, Zoya said. But as we got closer, we heard screams, deathly screams that curdle the blood in your veins. There was blood everywhere and the smell of burnt skin was nauseating. People were running about in no particular direction. Zoya and Mehr started crying out loud for Abba and Ammi. I was crying too but fear was an even greater overriding factor.

We ran towards our home. It had been burnt down just like every other house in the village. We asked Khader Uncle, our neighbour, if he had seen Abba and Ammi. He was hysterical.

'They have slaughtered my son. They have killed him.' There were hardly any men around. It was then that we saw five soldiers or more coming towards us. My first instinct was to run. I screamed at Zoya and Mehr to run as well. But they weren't aware of what was going to happen. I ran like I had never done before in my life, without turning to look back. I climbed a tamarind tree away from the chaos and hid between the leaves and branches. But even from there, I could see Zoya and Mehr being dragged onto a spot nearby. Their screams echoed everywhere. They were being stripped and beaten like savages. I put my hand over my mouth so that my cries would not be heard. They were being hounded. One soldier after another took turns violating them. I saw one of them beating Mehr with a wooden log and then raping her again. The more my sisters screamed, the more they tortured them. It went on for hours. I cried until I had no more tears. After a while, when the silence of the night fell like a death knell, I climbed down and lost consciousness from the exhaustion. My mind had shut down. I could not register what was happening. It was dark when I woke up. Ismael, our kitten, was sitting next to me. I held him close and hugged him and cried some more. In my mind, I knew this night marked the end of our journey and the beginning of another.

It was quiet outside the village. There was a power outage like on most nights. Only, tonight it wasn't going to come back. The local electricity board did that. Whenever there was trouble, they would disrupt power supply. I wonder now if it was to enable the army to do whatever they wanted to the people. The village looked like a ghost town. Ashes and embers were all that lingered. The smell of burnt bodies was in the air. Zoya and Mehr were in each other's arms, still asleep. My beautiful sisters. Tears rolled down my cheeks. I didn't want to wake them. Better to let them rest, or perhaps I was too much of a coward to face them. Somewhere in the distance, the radio was playing the 'Kyo' song. It was echoing in the air as if to placate the victims of the violence. The sound of that music will always haunt me, reminding me of the terror we faced that day. Even today, it triggers a deep sense of melancholia and despair within me.

When Zoya and Mehr finally woke up, they were different people. It was as if God had given life to the dead. The horrors of last evening were embalmed in their bodies. I wondered what they thought. Both had a vacant look in their eyes, and tears were streaming down their face incessantly. 'It's okay, Aapa. It's okay.' Those were the only words I could utter. Language eluded me. That or a part of my brain stopped processing. Grief does that to you. And loss. We had lost so many of our own that we had lost count.

I saw Mrs Noor from a distance. I ran up to her, hugged her and cried. She too, I guess, was in shock. We all were. The whole village knew what had happened to young girls last night. It was a collective shame that we would all have to carry for the rest of our lives. Mrs Noor took the three of us to a building close by, where many women, men and children were huddled. I saw a dozen men dressed in uniform standing guard outside. They had guns with them. 'Don't worry, Mohsina. They are with the ARSA (Arakan Rohingya Salvation Army). They will protect us.'

'I want to see Abba and Ammi, Miss,' I said, still crying.

'There are so many missing. That includes your Ammi and Abba. Now is not the time for tears. You need to be strong. You have to take care of your sisters. They need you. Tears will only make us weak. I have a plan. But we can carry it out only if you have the strength and resolve, Mohsina. Do you understand what I am saying? I am there for all of you. From now on, I am your family.' I held on to her tight, poured all the pain inside me into a shrill cry. I cried until I could cry no more. I had to be strong. We had no alternatives. 'Tears make us weak; they haul us down.' Mrs Noor's words rang in my head forever.

The events of the previous evening were too excruciating for us to process. The enormity of our loss was yet to be realized by our traumatized minds. Our parents were missing. Most of the huts in the villages were burnt down. Our neighbour Abbas' entire family was burnt to death inside the hut. The Burmese soldiers had locked them from outside. Several such houses were torched that way. But no one could find any such remains inside our home. There were rumours that the soldiers had taken several villagers hostage. Many were missing. People walked around like madmen. They were hysterical.

The shelter was as much a haven for us to experience collective grief as it was a place to gather and deconstruct. Mrs Noor took Zoya and Mehr inside a room. There was a doctor there from another village who examined them and dressed their wounds. She took them into a common bathroom, bathed them and gave them new clothes to wear. She told them never to think of what had happened to them as something to mourn and waste their lives over. 'It didn't happen to you, it happened to someone else,' she said. 'You must erase it completely from your memory. This is not how your story ends. This is where it begins. Do you get what I am saying?' Mehr and Zoya nodded. I watched Mrs Noor in amazement. She was so unassumingly strong, and the entire village depended on her.

After that day, we never talked about the incident. It was easier to move on that way. I guess most of us who have gone through extreme trauma cope through this sense of disassociation. In a way, we train our memory to turn those events into an out-of-body experience. As if it happened to someone else. It wasn't our problem.

I tagged along everywhere with Mrs Noor, attending to the ill, feeding the children, helping out in the kitchen, and sometimes even sitting guard outside the shelter. Nights were long and cold. We hardly slept those days. I looked out for Mehr and Zoya. I became a constant source of comfort and strength for them. Insomnia had become a forever companion.

◆

Tanya: There were 30 of them inside the shelter, including the ARSA guards. Men had separate rooms and women and children had a different one. It was overcrowded and smelt of urine and faeces. The ARSA members, it was rumoured, were recruited from the villages by a mysterious foreigner who went by the name of Ayatollah. He created his army to fight the Burmese Army's atrocities. They claimed to be an ethno-nationalist insurgent group, not jihadist. The boys and men who were recruited were taken to training camps at the Bangladesh–Pakistan border, where they were trained by Afghan and Pakistani fighters. The men then slipped back undetected to several villages, armed with basic ammunition and weapons. The core ideology of the ARSA was to preserve the rights of the Rohingyas and protect them.

Mohsina: One day, Mrs Noor came to us. She appeared deeply afraid. 'Leave everything. Carry only your absolute essentials and get ready to leave.'

'But where are we going?' Mehr asked.

'Questions later. Just pack and do as I tell you. Get the others ready as well.'

We rushed out carrying bare essentials. By the time everyone had assembled, two trucks carrying poultry arrived. It was stinking of poo. I felt nauseous. 'We have to somehow cope with a long journey staying hidden inside these trucks,' Mrs Noor addressed us. 'The Army is coming for us. We have news that they are combing through every village, and they are going to kill us all this time. These trucks will be a good hideout until we reach Buthidaung village. From there, we will need to trek through the Mayu mountains to reach Maungdaw district. We will hide in the forests during the day, and at night we will walk up to the Naf river, from where a ferry will take us across the border to Cox's Bazar in Bangladesh. Crossing over to Bangladesh relief camps is our only hope now. If we stay here, we won't live. They will make sure that none of us do.' She saw fear in our eyes. I guess she knew in her heart that only the strongest among us would survive this journey. 'We must keep silent. It is vital that we don't catch anyone's attention.'

My sisters and I got into the first truck. The drivers were of mixed-race descent, Indian and Burmese, but looked Burmese. Once we were inside, they placed the remaining cages on the exterior, so that no one would notice. They spoke fluent Burmese and were our lifeline for escape.

◆

Transcript #4

Mohsina: It took us three days to reach the town of Khin Tha Ma. We were stopped several times on the way by the army and Buddhist monks. We would hold our breath lest even the slightest sound or movement gave us away. Mehr, Zoya and I tried our best to organize our food rations so that we wouldn't run out. But even the best of our plans was derailed when a 65-year-old man travelling with us ran out of water and we had to share. Mrs Noor was losing energy. She fell ill on the way with diarrhoea and vomiting and was nearing a state of dehydration. The guards assured us that there was a small stream further up the road and that people often stopped there to drink water. It was a well-known stopover point. The drivers were sceptical but agreed.

It was 4.00 a.m. on the third day of our journey when we reached the pit stop near the stream. A few ARSA guards took everyone's bottles for a refill. The rest of us waited in the truck. It was still dark outside and terribly cold. I sat near Mrs Noor, nursing her and giving her water so that she wouldn't deteriorate further. We were down to two bottles, with 15 of us in the truck. We saw four of the guards returning with the bottles. They were just a few metres away when two of them fell on the ground and began frothing from the mouth. The other guards started shouting, trying to revive them. They did not make it. There was a lot of confusion. The drivers began screaming at the guards to get in. 'It's the water. It's poisoned,' screamed one of them. We guessed that the army had got to know that the stream was a stopover point for fleeing refugees, and poisoned it. The lengths they went to, to wipe us out, terrified and haunted us.

My heart began to sink. My sister, Mrs Noor and the children needed to be rehydrated quickly. They would not make it otherwise. I had no clue what to do. The truck reeked of vomit and stool. We were once more on the road. Without food and now without water. Our lips were parched and our throats dry. Our eyes stung because of the dryness. None of us spoke to each other, trying to save our energies. The drivers told us it would be just a few hours until we reached Buthidaung village. We could get medicines, food and water there. Those few hours were like years. I held Zoya close, running my fingers through her hair and singing her favourite *tarana*s. She was like a child, while at eighteen, I felt forty years old. I had taken a vow that no matter what the cost, I was going to be there for my sisters. We may have lost our parents, but we were not going to lose each other. I was determined.

By the time we reached Buthidaung township, we were exhausted. The lack of food, water and sunlight had made most of us sick. The trucks stopped near a forest outside the village, where we had to walk a bit to reach a campsite. A few of us had to carry Mrs Noor, who was too weak to even move. The drivers in the meantime went into the village that they were familiar with and got us provisions. We were to resume the journey within two days. Hopefully we would regain our strength by then. They left us in Kin Taung village, which was literally a ghost town. They wished us well.

My focus was on getting Mrs Noor and Zoya healthy again before we went on foot. The trek was going to be long and laborious. We needed all the strength we could muster. Mehr and I went around the forest and picked edible fruits that grew in the wild. I remembered Ammi making a juice out of them when we had stomach flu as kids. I did the same for Mrs Noor and Zoya. Within a day, both were feeling better and gaining strength but were in no position to cross the border by trekking. It would be at least two days before we could move.

The journey was long and arduous. The rest of the group was far ahead. We took our time, adjusting our pace so that Zoya and Mrs Noor could cope. The forest floor was marshy. A good pair of boots were a must to scale such a terrain, which we didn't have. One of the guards, Mahmoud, showed us the map that detailed our destination. Crossing the Mayu range would take us two days. And from there, we had to get to Maungdaw and head towards the Naf riverbank. A ferry would be waiting to take us to the Bangladesh border. Mehr and Zoya sighed. I could see that they were afraid.

Mahmoud, the ARSA soldier who was guiding us through the terrain, seemed reserved and distant. He looked very different from anyone I had ever seen. He had grey eyes, almost silver-grey. The kind of eyes that if you looked long enough into, you could drown in them. He took out a large jute cloth, cut it into square pieces and asked us to tie the scraps around our feet and legs. This would protect us from the marsh, insects and, God forbid, unwary reptiles. Mahmoud led the way and used sickles to cut the dense bushes that marked our path. He and I were carrying most of the provision baggage.

Mahmoud must have been around thirty. He hardly spoke and was always vigilant about the sights and sounds around him. I guess his training made him suspicious of anything even remotely unusual. He told us to maintain silence throughout our journey, to avoid the attention not only of wild animals that inhabited the mountain range but also of the Burmese Army. The army concentrated in these regions had many combing operations, as the ARSA was suspected to have training camps in the mountains.

He looked quite foreign but spoke fluent Ruanggia. I wondered what had brought him here. He seemed very serious about his mission, which was to ensure that we reached the Naf on time. I wondered what compelled fighters like him from other countries to put themselves in the line of fire just so that they could protect people like us? I couldn't help but admire that.

We followed him, Mehr and I supporting Mrs Noor most of the way. She looked like a ghost. Her pale skin was now an ashen grey. Her eyes were hollow. The dehydration was taking its toll. We stopped to give her the rehydration fluid that we had bought in the village.

'At this pace, it will take at least two days to reach Maungdaw.'

'We can't walk any faster,' I retorted. 'We have two sick people with us.'

Mahmoud looked at me with an air of arrogance. As if to say that that was not his problem. The jute cloth we had tied on our feet made it impossible to get a firm grip on the ground. At one point, Mehr slipped and fell along a slope. Luckily, there were no bruises or broken bones. We were too tired by the end of the day. The sun was setting, and we had no energy to move on even if Mahmoud insisted. 'We can't anymore. If we are to die, then let us,' Zoya cried.

'There is a shelter a little further ahead. More like a hideout. We can rest there for the night.'

The shelter was a hollow cave, covered with branches and leaves for camouflage. There was hardly any place to move. But the four of us had to somehow manage for the night.

There was a beautiful stream nearby. Its crystal-clear water was beckoning me. How I wished to bathe in it. My body was smelling of sweat and dirt, the skin had tanned and turned darker, and my hair a colour of burnt wood. Perhaps when the sun set and it grew darker, I could take that bath.

Mahmoud had bought some rice, biscuits and bread from the village. He collected a few twigs and relatively dry leaves and made a fire. With rice and water, he made *konji* for us. After the long trek of almost five hours, it was the most delicious thing on my lips. I smiled in gratitude. He did likewise. After everyone fell asleep, I tiptoed out. The stream was just a few feet away from the shelter, hidden by tall trees that surrounded it. The full moon left a trail of light leading to the water. I was scared for a while, wondering if wild animals would be around. But the need to feel water on my parched skin superseded every caution. I took off my clothes and let my body soak in the cold water. It reached my waist. I dipped my head into it and let my senses drown in the beauty of silence that surrounded me. Just then, I felt something pull my arm violently. I was about to scream when a hand cupped my mouth.

'Not a word! You have no idea how you have jeopardized us. You could have had us all killed, stupid girl!' It was Mahmoud. He dragged me to the shore. I was left standing naked in front of him.

'I felt sick. I needed to have a wash,' I said feebly.

'We can't have that luxury now. Don't you get it? Those men are swarming the forests. There's no telling.'

I stood there quivering, the cold breeze humming in my ear. 'I am sorry,' I mumbled. He hesitantly handed me the clothes that I had carelessly left on the ground, his grey eyes piercing my skin, and the next thing I knew, he pulled me close and kissed me ferociously. I didn't resist. His hands were all over me, touching my skin, digging into my bones. Wherever he touched, there was a trail of a neon purple glow. Like a constellation. A galaxy. My mind was playing tricks on me, or perhaps it was the moon glowing over the forest that was to blame. I wasn't sure. His grey eyes turned silver, and his breath smelt of sea water. I should have been scared. Everything seemed so unusual. He didn't look human. But I didn't care. Here I was at eighteen years of age, almost losing my virginity to a stranger, a soldier in fact, who right now held our lives in his hands. I felt indebted to him. His fair hands were like an albino spider hungrily traversing the length of my dusky skin, leaving a trail of incandescence. What an amazing work of art we must have looked if someone saw us. He murmured my name as he left no place unexplored. Fear, I realized that day, was a potent aphrodisiac. We made love twice that night and returned to the shelter only when it was dawn.

When I woke up in the morning, I had no clue if what had happened the previous night was all a dream. I felt so disoriented. It seemed so surreal. Then I looked at the marks on my thighs and back, glittering red scars left by the gravel and slush on the ground. I was so nervous and shy about facing Mahmoud again. There were far too many questions than answers. The happiness and fear were real. Mehr and Zoya were ready by the time I woke up. Mrs Noor seemed much better in the morning. I thought she seemed kind of lost. She looked at me in a strange way. I wondered if she knew or suspected…

Mahmoud was in a friendlier, more relaxed frame of mind that morning. He stole glances at me when I wasn't looking. Mehr and Zoya laughed at what seemed like a blooming love story right in front of their eyes. I was too young, too naïve to think anything except being swept away by this euphoric feeling inside my head. 'We have six more hours of walking ahead of us, until we reach Maungdaw. The rest of the team would have reached there by now. A few of them, in all probability, are on their way to Bangladesh across the Naf,' Mahmoud said in a nonchalant manner. How handsome he looked, I thought to myself. His eyes and aquiline features were like that of a Roman king. I wondered what our children would look like. I was holding Mrs Noor's hand and helping her along the way. The illness had made her quite weak.

'Do you think Abba and Ammi are alive?' I asked her.

'I wish I could tell you, my dear. Just as I wish I could about the 150 people that went missing that night. I am hoping that they are somewhere safe. That they ran away and reached the Naf and are waiting for us on the other side. I wish I could tell you that.' I cried a little. What were the chances, I asked myself.

'Mohsina, do you realize tomorrow, by the afternoon, we will be on our way to Cox's Bazar?'

'Yes, Mrs Noor, and Inshallah, we will have an opportunity to start a new life there,' I said, smiling at her.

'Yes, but do you realize that we will be leaving behind the life we have known here and everyone in it?'

I understood what she was trying to say. In many ways, Mrs Noor could read my mind. She knew me even better than I knew myself. I knew she was trying to tell me to not allow my past or Mahmoud enter my thoughts. Because there will be separation even before we begin to know each other. My sisters and I had lost so much in Sittwe. My chest felt heavy like a clenched soul. I wanted to know more about Mahmoud before we said goodbye. I ran ahead to walk beside him.

The sun was scorching above us. The Mayu mountaintop was more barren than the slope during the ascent. Our skin was tanned beyond recognition, lips were parched and broken, and our feet hurt. By now, none of us were wearing footwear. It didn't survive the rough terrain. All that sort of stuff didn't matter. We were all consumed by our end goal. To get away. Yet for me, love had happened along the way. I wish it hadn't since it was taking away my focus.

'So, where are you from, Mr Glow Man?' I teased him.

'I would request you to not persist with that query,' he said, seeming oblivious to my presence.

'Not persist? Something happened last night, or have you forgotten?' I was getting irritable due to his lack of attention.

'I don't forget anything,' he said, looking at me, 'and yet your question is of no consequence and is irrelevant.'

'Maybe not to you but to me it is. I don't get why you seem irked today. Are you trying to suggest that I should forget whatever happened last night? I am not even sure if I will make it out there. The least you can do is feign love.' I was in tears.

'Wipe your tears. You don't want others to see us.' He looked behind. Zoya, Mehr and Mrs Noor were a few metres away.

'I don't care who knows. I can't believe that what we shared last night means nothing to you. Is this a part of your job? To fuck refugee girls during their passage?'

He stopped in his tracks and would have slapped me had I not been a woman. Instead, he clenched his jaws and glared at me for a few seconds. 'I am sorry for what happened last night. It shouldn't have. But it did. I broke the rules. My people will never forgive me for this. You think I don't feel bad? I am not like you, Mohsina. Never will be like you. Do you get what I am saying? We are a tribe quite different from you all. Half-human, half-divine, we are born out of intense *ruhaniyat*. You must have heard about us. The Khanabadosh, the gypsy soul wanderers, the warriors of light!'

I couldn't believe what I was hearing. It was like listening to one of Mrs Noor's fairytales. She would tell us amazing mystical stories about the Khanabadosh. Stories of valour and courage. Tribesmen and women who stood with the underdogs, the poor and the oppressed. Right now, I couldn't believe what I was hearing.

'Really, Mahmoud?' I pinched his arm in disbelief, my anger completely dissipating.

'Yes, Mohsina, unbelievable but true.'

I felt I was living a fairytale.

'What is ruhaniyat?'

'It's a state of deep, sublime soulfulness. It happens when a human and a *ruh*, or spirit, from the netherworld fall in love. And in that state of intense connection, they make love. It is an act of transcendence and far beyond the realm of human understanding. The Sufis are known to be aware of this divine revelation. And out of this union, the Khanabadosh are born. The Khanabadosh are very few in number—60,000, to be precise—and scattered across the world. We have distinct features like our silver-grey eyes and the ability to emanate that neon purple glow when we are in a state of excitement or agitation, which you witnessed when we made love. This is our present form. Those more evolved amongst us are far more powerful— for instance, they can regenerate from fatal wounds, morph their appearance and disappear at will. We live very long—actually, we die when we choose to. Our tribe has been in existence since as early as man himself. You must have heard about a few of our forefathers. They have all been a part of this universe to save humanity from itself. Our mission is to fight the good fight. To help humanity find their ruhaniyat and in turn, we choose peace and love over terror and war. Sometimes, to achieve those goals, we may also have to fight the dark forces, labour in a war between the persecuted and the persecutors. My assignment was in Rakhine. Which brought me to you. Serendipity, don't you think?'

I didn't know what to think or believe. All those details were like an information overload for my 18-year-old mind. I didn't say anything. I was in awe of his handsome face that had a beautiful aura.

'No one knows about us. Maintaining utmost secrecy is crucial. Otherwise, it would wreak havoc for the Khanabadosh. Do you get what I am saying, Mohsina?' I nodded quietly, with tears in my eyes. I did not want to waste a single moment that I had with him. In my mind, I knew we had very little time.

'We have allegiance only to our ideological faith. To nothing and no one else. Our purpose is towards the decree of the Supreme Being. Humans have undone the balance. We are the chosen ones to restore it. We have to remain emotionally detached if we want to be victorious in this war. Yet I succumbed to my human desire and instincts, seeing how beautiful and vulnerable you looked under that moonlight in the water. I am sorry for that.'

I felt my heart sink. I knew how hopeless this was. He, a half-human insurgent soldier, and I, a soon-to-be refugee. Even by luck, what were our chances? Yet I had chosen love over everything else.

'It's okay. I understand. I just hoped…'

'Hoped what, Mohsina?' I didn't have answers or maybe I thought it futile to answer. We resumed walking as we started the descent down the mountain.

He waved to Mehr, Zoya and Mrs Noor. 'The terrain is much drier and more effortless on this side of the mountain as we descend. But do be careful,' he spoke Rohingya so fluently that anyone would have been fooled.

I wiped my face and looked ahead. From atop, we could see the Naf, coursing through the valley like a snake. 'That is Bangladesh. Just across the river on the other side. Looks so easy, doesn't it?' Mahmoud pointed it out to me and smiled. I refused to smile back, looking the other way instead. He held my hand as we climbed down the range.

The descent from Mayu was much easier than we had thought. We rested a while to eat and hydrate ourselves. The hot sun burnt everything it could—the trees, the leaves, even the soil beneath our feet. As it did our souls. We built a shelter with twigs and leaves when night descended. Mahmoud told us we were just half an hour away from Maungdaw.

'We will rest here tonight. Around 4.00 a.m. we will go towards the village, to the riverbank, when it is still dark. The ferry will leave by 5.00 a.m. And by six, you will be at the Bangladesh border, Inshallah.'

It was 11.00 p.m. by the time everyone slept. I went outside the cave where Mahmoud was sitting guard and sat beside him. He looked at me with those eyes that would haunt me forever. I rested my head on his shoulders and began to cry.

'Will you come with us to the other side?'

'I can't, Mohsina.' He held my face.

'You could help people at the refugee camps too. I hear

there's a lot of work that needs to be done there as well.'

'But not as crucial as it is here.'

'So I guess this is goodbye?' I couldn't control my tears. Was it possible to fall in love in just a day?

'You will endure and emerge triumphant, my love,' he said, as though he could read my mind. 'I am not sure if it is goodbye. The universe has plans that we don't know of. Who knows, maybe one day you will be able to summon me to your world?' He smiled.

'I don't have special powers, don't you know?'

'You never know, Mohsina.' His smile broadened.

I kissed him then. And that night—for the last time—we made love. Holding on to each other for dear life. Even in absolute silence, I felt deeply connected. Perhaps this was my divine experience. They say everything happens for a reason. I wondered what ours was. We did not sleep a wink that night.

By 3.30 a.m., we got ready to leave and by 4.00 a.m., we were on our way, trepidation rocking our hearts. The five-kilometre stretch seemed to take forever. We looked at each other nervously as we entered the village. Mahmoud talked to us in cues. It was still pitch-dark. The ferry would be waiting at the banks of the Naf. It was merely a few minutes away.

I walked through the streets beside Mahmoud. Just then, we heard shots fired from the trees. Mahmoud motioned us to run into the sugarcane fields along the road. We heard more shots and then screams of men getting closer.

'Comb the area,' we heard someone say. At that moment in time, we were in fight-or-flight mode. I felt no fear. Just this raging need to stay alive. Mahmoud signalled us to stay put and not move even an inch. Just then, we heard footsteps near us. And in one fleeting moment, a soldier emerged in front of us, and in the next, Mahmoud swooped down upon him and stabbed him with a knife. We had to hurry. The road was clear. The four soldiers who fired the shots were still in the fields looking for us. 'Run!' he told us, 'We are almost there!'

We ran for our lives and after a few hundred metres, we saw the clear waters of the mysterious Naf. The riverbank was a long stretch. And just then, from a distance, we saw a small catamaran emerging, hidden by the waves. It was 5.45 a.m., and the sun was just rising. We were all in too much of a hurry and panic to get into the rickety catamaran. I stood there, the last one to get in, refusing to let go for a few seconds more. 'Mohsina, get in now. Go!' Mahmoud was shouting. I ran towards him, and he kissed me for what we knew would be the last time. 'Go, my love. Please leave. They will be here any moment, and you won't have a chance.'

I was crying. I left him and ran towards the catamaran, my teardrops merging with the waters of the Naf. My sisters dragged me into the boat. From a distance, I could see soldiers firing shots at us. By then, we were at a safe distance from the shore. I looked out for Mahmoud but couldn't see him anywhere. He had vanished. Just like that. I wondered if the soldiers had caught him or if he had disappeared like he said he could. It all seemed like a surreal dream. I held onto my sisters and Mrs Noor and cried. The sun was scorching, and we were halfway along the Naf. The catamaran was small and rickety, wobbling against the waves. We should have been overjoyed. We were reclaiming our lives. Yet there was a sense of foreboding, as if this was a journey that would never end. As if the battle had just begun.

◆

Inspector Angami paused for a while. He looked at his watch. There was still an hour and a half to touchdown at Delhi, yet it seemed like a lifetime. He was preoccupied with Mohsina's story. His heart felt heavy. He had heard so many things about the Rohingyas. A few had managed to get to Nagaland from the refugee camps in New Delhi and West Bengal. There were reports of unrest created by local Naga villagers, blaming the refugees for the rising crime rate in the district. The police had to intervene to prevent outbreaks of violence. He felt sorry for them—these stateless ones who were turned away from their own country as well as those where they sought refuge. This was the plight of refugees everywhere. Xenophobia was on the rise the world over, and so were right-wing governments. With civil wars raging in several countries, the number of the displaced was close to 65 million! He sighed wondering about the human condition.

Angami clicked on the next transcript. Mohsina's story had him engrossed.

4

Transcript #5

Mohsina: As the boat inched closer to the shore along the Bangladesh border, the landscape reminded me so much of Myanmar. We disembarked at the shore. I still felt disoriented. The separation from Mahmoud was still heavy on my mind. The journey had been arduous, even dangerous. The waters of the Naf are infamous for their unpredictability. But we were lucky. The weather was in our favour and so were the river gods.

We would have to walk quite some more to reach Palong Kali village, the fisherman told us. A lot of local buses shuttled between the village and Cox's Bazar, where most of the refugee camps were located. It was a very short distance but extremely marshy. We needed all the strength we could muster. We were almost there.

The narrow marshlands between the mangroves and the bushes were very difficult to navigate. Every step was an effort. Yet we persisted. Finally, after walking a few kilometres, we stopped near a water body that passed through the mangroves. We could see a few other people walking far ahead of us. It was Uncle Hakim, Uncle Abdul and their families. They used to live a few huts away from ours in Sittwe. They had boarded the second truck when we all fled.

There were in total ten of our old neighbours. 'We reached last night. None of us had any energy to walk up to Palong

Kali. So we rested on the banks until the morning. We were just relieved that we could get away from the horror of the past few days. I am sorry your families didn't make it,' Uncle Hakim said, crying.

'We are each other's family now, Hakim Bhai,' Mrs Noor told him.

By the grace of the universe, we reached Palong Kali within an hour, tired and hungry. There were dozens of men waiting on the top of the slope to lift us from the knee-deep slushy waters and onto the shore. My lungi and shirt were totally wet and full of dirt. I felt as if my feet were embedded deep into the marsh bed, and I just didn't have the strength to climb out. Two men had to hold my hand and literally pull me out.

'Welcome to Bangladesh,' they cheered jubilantly. I will never forget how those three words made me feel. It was like a balm soothing our tired souls and battered bodies. Mrs Noor spoke to them. It was uncanny how similar we looked to the Banglas; we even spoke like them. The men, like ours, were dressed in lungis, had dark skin too. Two people divided by a border who still felt a kinship. I realized then how vital it was to have a shared history, religion and even DNA for people to feel that sense of belongingness. I wondered, and still do, if this was how immigrants felt everywhere? Never belonging to their adopted countries no matter what.

For some reason, despite the near hypoglycaemic state and the weariness of our journey, we already felt as if we had come home. They gave us food and water as soon as we arrived and took us to a makeshift bathroom where we could clean ourselves and wear new clothes that they gave us. I was extremely touched by their kindness. We hadn't known what that felt like for a long time.

All fourteen of us felt as if we were born again, in another place and time. For the first time in days, we were smiling. I felt this overwhelming love and sadness for my people. We were poor but our hearts were pure. By the time the bus arrived to take us to Cox's Bazar, it was 2.00 p.m. Everyone was excited. Slowly but surely, as hope glimmered, we allowed ourselves the luxury of contrary emotions—laughter and tears.

By the time we arrived at Cox's Bazar, it was 5.00 p.m. Two men, Ashraf and Hameed, spoke to us at length on what to expect. Cox's Bazar apparently had two refugee camps, Kutupalong and Nayapara. There were also many makeshift settlements on the outskirts of the town, they said. The makeshift camps had very basic facilities. Kutupalong was one of the largest and had 34,000 refugees. The United Nations had set up schools, private clinics and provision stores at the camp. It was only later that we learnt what the UN was. I first met Tanya Di when she was part of the UNHCR volunteer media team.

As we crossed the Cox's Bazar border, the first thing that struck us were the acres and acres of dwellings made of tin sheet, wood and plastic roof that covered the landscape. There were no spaces between the houses, and it seemed as if an entire sea of humanity had descended there. There were children running around, and from the foul smell in the air, it was obvious that the sewage system was in shambles. People lived among death and disease. It was intimidating. For a moment, I missed my home in Sittwe. The green open spaces and crystal-clear waters. What I wouldn't have done to go back. But I knew that that was never an option. Memory that way can be cruel. This longing for something which never was nor will be ours.

'It's not going to be easy,' Hameed said as if reading my thoughts. 'But Bangladesh itself is short on resources, and this is what we are doing to help, with a lot of assistance from organizations like the UNHCR. It will take a while for your houses to get ready. Until then, the fourteen of you will have to make do in a temporary shelter just at the border of the camp.' Everyone nodded as if they understood. These things mattered so little. When your very existence is threatened, all you want is a safe place; it does not matter how big or comfortable it is.

By the time we entered the camp premises, it was dark. The houses were illuminated by kerosene lamps. Children were still playing outside. Hameed told us that 60 per cent of the inhabitants were children whose families had been taken away or murdered by the Burmese Army. Somewhere I could hear a child singing a song that had become a recognizable folk tune to every Rohingya who grazed carefree in his fields back home in Rakhine.

We are Arakans.
Our eyes are weeping.
Why is your luck not changing?
Oh, Rohingya people!

The child's song brought a flood of memories that I could not contain. Zoya held me tight.

'Let it go,' she said. 'Let it all go and then when you are done, we will go back to rebuilding our lives. Remember what Mrs Noor said. Let's not allow our feelings to control our lives. If we are to make it in this lifetime, Mohsina, we need to be strong as the metal on a hot tin roof. Blazing under the sun, yet not melting. We need to do whatever it takes for us to survive.'

It was dark and there were mosquitoes. The stench of an open sewer somewhere made us balk. I looked at my sisters. My heart went out to them. Both had gone through such horrific circumstances, yet they were so strong. Like my sister said, 'They can only scar our bodies, not our minds.' I hugged her and fell asleep on the mat.

Morning came with the reality of how life would be at the camp. At 5.00 a.m., Zoya, Mehr and I went up to the community water pump to collect water for our shelter. Each of us had two buckets with us. It would barely be enough to see us through the day. The queue was too long. A few people who had been living in the camps for years gave us advice on life in Kutupalong.

'Try to find a job. Any job. There is a local school close by. I heard they are looking for volunteers.'

'Out here in Kutupalong, you need to work to feed yourself and your family.'

'Stay away from strange men who come to you with offers of work or marriage. These are pimps. They lure our girls and women for sinister purposes. They all make money but lose their souls. Look at Ayesha there, the one in the green saree. Isn't she pretty? She is what they call a *chukri* or a bonded girl. She has been one since she was fourteen. Everything comes at a cost, and it is rumoured these girls become diseased as well. Just stay away from them.'

My eyes followed Ayesha. She was so different from the rest of us. Even at 6.00 a.m. in the morning, she was overdressed. She was chewing betel leaves and occasionally spat out, causing much irritation to the other women nearby. She laughed loudly at their apparent disgust. There was seduction even in her laughter. She hardly looked nineteen, yet her body looked like that of a 30-year-old. We were terrified by her fate and hoped and prayed we would remain safe.

◆

Mrs Noor was in charge of managing our home, House No. 505. One day, while washing clothes in a canal close by, I asked Mrs Noor if we could work too rather than depending on Uncle Hakim and Uncle Abdul, who got a pittance as labourers. It wasn't fair that we asked them to take care of us too.

'The thought did pass through my mind, Mohsina. I thought we would wait until we settled a bit.'

There was a school nearby and there was a vacancy for teachers. They paid a decent amount: 300 taka per week. It was run by the UNHCR. The interview was by a kind white lady from Sweden who was volunteering. Mrs Noor and I were selected because we could read and speak English and Bangla. Zoya got a job as a nanny at the school daycare. Mehr eventually got a job outside the settlement.

'One day, we will be able to fly out of Cox's Bazar to India or even to the UK or US—anywhere. I have calculated everything. There are a lot of people in the West who understand and empathize with the Rohingyas. We can build a better life there.' Mehr's eyes would always light up when she talked about our future. The pay wasn't as much as we expected. But it was enough to keep us afloat for a while.

I knew that Cox's Bazar was not our haven. It was our temporary transit. In my heart, I knew we needed other options. I believed that an opportunity would present itself someday. We began getting comfortable with routine life in Kutupalong. Days turned into weeks and weeks into months. It was hard to imagine it had been two months already. We spent our lives between school and home. Life seemed to have found some semblance of normality and mundaneness for the moment.

But then, as they say, man proposes, God disposes. All our plans were derailed. And I was solely responsible for this. One day, two months after we had landed in Cox's Bazar, I fell ill at school while in class. I vomited a lot and was on the verge of losing consciousness. They rushed me to the clinic close by and the doctor kept me there a while to monitor my condition and administer an IV drip. When I regained my senses, Mehr, Zoya and Mrs Noor were next to me.

'I feel better now. Can we go home?'

There was an awkward silence for some time.

'Mohsina, you are two months pregnant,' said Mrs Noor, matter-of-factly.

'What???' I couldn't believe what I was hearing. My head was spinning again.

Zoya held my hand. 'It's okay.'

'You have two choices, Mohsina,' Mrs Noor said in her usual pragmatic way. 'You can abort the child or keep it. The question is, are you ready? You are just eighteen, Mohsina. Your whole life is ahead of you. And with our meagre resources and living conditions, do you really want to bring a child into this world?'

I began to cry. I didn't know what to think. How could I make this decision? 'This child is the result of love. It's Mahmoud's. The child is the chosen one. Of the Khanabadosh tribe. I cannot commit murder.'

They fell silent again. Partly in shock and partly in disbelief, as they heard that Mahmoud was of Khanabadosh descent. My sisters were sceptical, but Mrs Noor seemed alarmed.

'Then it puts us all in even greater danger. We will have to be very, very careful. Even a whisper that this unborn child is of one of them can put you and the baby in peril. The Khanabadosh have enemies, powerful ones, everywhere,' Mrs Noor warned us.

'She will keep the baby. We will find the means to support it. Don't worry about that. This secret will live and die with the four of us.' Mehr was adamant.

We all nodded in silence. It was unbelievable. But how could it not be? This was a fait accompli. Our destiny. And our baby was destiny's child. I was willing to risk it all for him or her.

No one at the camp asked about my pregnancy. There were many unwed or widowed mothers. Many of them were rape victims; there were others whose husbands had been captured or killed. They had no means to abort and some of them didn't want to. It had become a way of life. A whole generation without fathers. I wondered what would become of them all.

When Qismet was born, there was a thunderstorm that night. Zoya ran outside to call the midwife. It poured profusely and drenched the parched earth. The children ran out of their homes and danced in the rain. I could smell the earth, and its calming presence embraced me. My sisters, Mrs Noor and other ladies were huddled around me. The midwife was ordering them to get this or that. All I could focus on was the unbearable pain that was coursing through my body. Mehr held my hand tight. As I screamed one last time, the cries of the little one mingled with mine. A part of Mahmoud would always be with me now. I remembered his parting words.

Our miraculous destiny's child—Qismet. Yes, that would be our child's name. When I held him in my arms, tears fell effortlessly. I was in love once more—the chosen one with black hair and silver-grey eyes, just like his father. In my mind, I promised to guard him with my life.

The birth of Qismet brought much joy into our lives. Everyone in Kutupalong came to see him. They were curious about him. His eyes were so different from those of the other children. Someone remarked that they reminded them of a rainstorm. No, a snowstorm, someone else said. I was worried that *buri nazar* would befall my child and harm him. But the love and affection kept pouring in.

Qismet grew under strict surveillance. He started walking by the time he was three months old. And he talked in full sentences by the time he was six months. Now these were things we could not hide. As much as we tried to portray him as a *normal* child, his rare skills would soon become the talk of Kutupalong. I wished Mahmoud were here. I wouldn't have worried so much. One day, on a clear summer night, I sat outside our hut, with Qismet fast asleep in my arms. I looked at the sky and focused on the constellations. It looked so beautiful. Orion, the Hunter, in particular. I was unsure of what lay ahead for us. If only I had the power to protect Qismet. It was so beautiful and quiet that night. The summer breeze brought some respite. My baby looked like an angel as he slept in my arms. He was of divine birth. That he had to grow up in the refugee slums of Kutupalong was unfair. I held my son closer. At that moment, I knew I had to escape Cox's Bazar to somewhere safer for him.

'Don't worry, Mohsina, you will know what to do when it's time.'

I turned back, startled. His voice was ringing in my ear. It was Mahmoud! I was certain of it. I called out to him. Several times. But he seemed nowhere around. Was it my imagination? Was I too stressed? I found a silver thread beside me. Instantly I knew what to do with it. I had seen it on Mahmoud too. I chanted the Fatiha and tied it to Qismet's hand. Mahmoud was here. He was watching over us. I could sense his presence. I cried out in happiness.

◆

Transcript #6

Mohsina: It was as if by serendipity that we met Tanya Singh at the school the following week. She was there as part of a documentary shoot with the UNHCR and was quite impressed with the work that we did with the school children. She spent a lot of time talking to us about Kutupalong and the events that had brought us here from Rakhine.

'There are about 700,000 refugees in Bangladesh alone, right now. It's an impossible task for the Bangladesh government to do this all alone. There are rumours that they are in talks with the Burmese government to relocate Rohingyas from the camps back to Rakhine,' she told Mrs Noor. The UNHCR was randomly selecting people to relocate them to India and other South Asian countries because the Bangladesh government was finding it increasingly difficult to look after the growing influx of refugees. We were on the list. It would take at least a few months, she said.

'I have a baby. I can't go back to Myanmar. They will murder him. Please take us away soon, ma'am. Please.' I fell at Didi's feet, almost hysterical.

She hugged me. It was as if a mother was holding her child. At that moment, our destinies were inexplicably entwined.

'I would if I could,' she said. 'But India is not a long-term solution for you at all. The current government is not very welcoming of the Rohingyas. They have already sealed the borders and refused to take anymore,' she said, looking at Mrs Noor. 'I am trying my best, however, to put pressure on the government through the UNHCR to sign the Refugee Convention. That would safeguard the Rohingyas and other refugees in India. I have a feeling that things will work out. Be strong.' She assured us before she left.

I lived with constant dread each day that someone would take Qismet away or we would be sent back to Sittwe. This constant fear of loss, of those you love, is always there like a gauntlet at the back of my mind. There was nothing I wouldn't do for them. I had lost my parents, friends and neighbours. I was not willing to lose anymore. I would even kill for those I loved.

When we did not hear from Tanya Didi for three months, we gave up hope. How we all sought refuge in one another. At least my sisters and I had each other. People like Mrs Noor had lost everything. Like most Rohingyas, she had no one to call her own except us. Her life was a perfect example of the loss a human heart could hold and some more.

◆

Qismet was a handsome child and had his father's eyes, hair and skin. People wondered who his Abba was. He was born with a beautiful red birthmark in the shape of a heart on his forehead. People sometimes called him *farishta*, or angel. When he started to talk around six months, everyone confirmed he was a blessed one. This love was overwhelming.

Rumours about the confidential pact that the Bangladesh government had with Myanmar to deport the refugees back to Myanmar started gaining momentum. One day, a few police officials came to our shelter and took Uncle Hakim and Uncle Abdul away. They came back after several hours around midnight, looking haggard. 'We will need to move back to Sittwe,' they said, breaking down. 'The women and children can stay, at least for now.'

Their wives cried aloud, beating their breasts as if to summon the spirits of Sittwe. Hearing this, the children began howling too. 'We are coming too,' they cried. 'What use are we if you are not by our side? How will we raise our children without their fathers? We are coming no matter where you go.'

I did not know what to do. It was heartbreaking. I had no idea why they were chosen to be deported. I guess it was because every male Rohingya was viewed as a potential ARSA terrorist or sympathizer. Just then, I heard footsteps and screaming outside. I looked out of the window to see what was going on. There were soldiers everywhere inspecting houses. At this hour? Alarm bells rang in my head. 'Where is the child?' a gravel voice ordered. Everyone ran out to see what the commotion was about. 'We have heard that there is a six-month-old child here in the neighbourhood, with silver-grey eyes who can talk as adults do. Is he in this house?'

My heart sank and my mind went numb. Qismet! They were searching for Qismet. I ran back into the house, quietly wrapped him in a towel, placed him in a basket and covered him with a jute cloth.

'Don't make a sound, my child. No harm will come to you.' He opened his eyes, smiled and went back to sleep, as if he understood every word I said.

Within a few moments, they were inside our home, intimidating us with questions and inspecting everywhere. I prayed fervently. They checked every nook and corner of the house except the basket. Everything was thrown upside down. They couldn't find a thing. I heaved a sigh of relief when they left. After a while, I removed the cloth and took him in my arms. He was sleeping peacefully.

'We have to leave now,' I said, almost hysterical.

'They are gone now. We will think this through and move forward,' Mehr said. 'One of our neighbours has a mobile phone. You have Tanya Didi's number, don't you? Let's talk to her.'

She got the cell phone and dialled.

Ring one, no answer.

Ring two, still no answer.

Ring three. 'Hello…' responded a sleepy voice at the other end of the line.

'Tanya Di. This is Mohsina.'

'Who?'

'Mohsina from Cox's Bazar. Remember you had met us here? I was with my baby. You promised to help us out of here?'

'Mohsina, what happened?' Tanya Di sounded distracted.

'Didi, they are randomly deporting people back to Myanmar. A hunt is on by the government authorities for the baby with grey eyes at the camp. My Qismet.'

'What? I think you are being paranoid. Bangladesh is bound by the Refugee Convention. They wouldn't do that. Not yet.'

'Didi, I need to tell you something more. I should have when you were here. But for some reason, I didn't.'

I briefly discussed Qismet's birth, Mahmoud and the

Khanabadosh. She was quiet for a long time. As though she could not make up her mind if I was delusional or making things up just to escape the camp. She said she had heard about the tribe but only as hearsay. She was deeply distressed when she hung up.

In a week's time, someone from the UNHCR came with passports and visas for the five of us. Our destination: Kohima, Nagaland, India. We were overjoyed. On the eve of our departure, Mrs Noor seemed more morose than usual at dinner. She said she did not want to leave.

Everyone fell silent for a while.

'We can't leave without you,' Mehr intervened.

'No. No. Listen to what I am trying to tell you. It is crucial that you leave. I am getting frail and old. I will only slow you down. It's a long journey, not just to India, but from there to elsewhere too. At my age, I am not fit enough physically or emotionally to bear that kind of change. I want to live the remaining part of my life here, in the Kutupalong camp, and help those who come here. The children need me. I cannot abandon them.'

'Please don't do this. We cannot go without you. We all go or none of us will.' I was on the verge of tears.

'Please don't be stubborn about this, Mohsina. It will only make me sad. I am happy here. Why should you give up Qismet's safety for my happiness? There awaits a better future for all of you. You always have my love and blessings.'

We did not want to leave Mrs Noor alone in Kutupalong. But Mrs Noor wanted to stay. That was her choice, and we had to respect that.

Meanwhile, inspections and raids for the child with the silver-grey eyes were still on in neighbouring shelters and camps. News travels fast. We heard rumours that the governments of many countries were on the lookout for the Khanabadosh. They were no longer legends but a reality. They were considered a threat to both military dictators and democracies. The Khanabadosh were not just warriors but whistleblowers too. They were the moral conscience of nations and societies that had lost theirs. I wondered if Qismet would be safe anywhere. Would I be able to raise him without a shadow of danger? Only time would tell.

It was heartbreaking to leave Mrs Noor behind. She was smiling and waving at us. 'We will come back for you,' I told her as I hugged her tight, with tears in my eyes.

'Inshallah, child. Take care of yourself and Qismet. Be brave.' She kissed my forehead. Nothing scared us anymore. We had been through hell and back, and could not be intimidated easily. Such was the strength of the spirits born of the mountains.

◆

Angami took a deep breath. He felt as if he was living Mohsina's life. Her narrative seeped into his conscious mind like water into a sponge. He was in awe of the resilient spirit of the refugees in the face of adversities. Of course, he had seen similar scenarios play out in riot-hit areas. Men, women and children moved on with their lives as if nothing had ever happened. Poverty does that to people. Survival is their only goal. It was the affluent who were unable to cope with life's adversities.

Angami began wondering about the Khanabadosh. Was it all a figment of Mohsina's mind? This sense of an altered reality. Post-traumatic stress disorder? You never know. He tried to google about the Khanabadosh but found nothing to ascertain their existence. All available material was mere speculation and information that everyone already knew. Conspiracy theories, Angami thought to himself. For some reason, he had a strong feeling that Tanya's death was related to Mohsina and her sisters' lives. He needed to track them down and meet them.

The pilot announced the descent and for once, Angami was relieved that it would all be over soon. He had a gut feeling that he was inching close to the truth.

Angami stretched his legs and looked at his watch. Another 45 minutes more to land in New Delhi.

∽∞∾

5

Zahira Choudhary, Tanya Singh's closest friend and perhaps the last person she spoke to on the phone, was not home when Angami arrived. The maid ushered the inspector into the well-furnished apartment.

'Madam will be back soon. *Chai ya* coffee, sir?'

'Nothing, thanks.'

He noticed that the lady had a distinct Bengali accent while speaking Hindi. She was wearing a lungi and kurta. He wondered if she was a Rohingya. Angami studied the apartment. Very plush with Middle Eastern décor. There were several pictures on the mantle. He examined them. Zahira was a beautiful woman. She was of Kashmiri descent. Her facial features made that obvious. There were several pictures with family and friends. Angami noticed a few with Tanya as well. He noticed that the pictures were from different stages of their lives: school, college, office and so on. There was one with Zahira, Tanya and Aman. Happy times. There was another one that caught his attention: a picture with Nick Kent, the photographer at Kohima, who was dressed as a head-hunter with a dao in his left hand, pretending to be a fierce warrior. Tanya and Zahira were laughing in the picture. Probably at Kent's antics. Kent had mentioned they had done a photo project together.

'That was on my first visit to Kohima. Tanya had insisted that I go during the Hornbill Festival. We had such a great time. Nick and Tanya were working together on the Headhunters Project at the time. A photo story.'

It was Zahira. Angami was pleasantly surprised to see her watching him. He hadn't realized she had come home.

'I apologize profusely, Inspector. I had intended to call you. But I was held up in the newsroom.'

'That's okay, ma'am.'

She tried to smile.

'Do you have any news about Tanya's killer?' Her voice was heavy. It broke a bit as she spoke. 'I still feel as if this is all just a bad nightmare.'

'Nothing concrete yet. I am still collecting evidence, talking to people, trying to put stuff together. Which is why I have come to you. I need to know a few things.'

'Will be glad to help, Inspector.'

'I have a pendrive with me. It's Tanya's. Aman said that she had wished to hand it over to you. There were many photographs, a few videos and a couple of journal entries. Do you have any idea what it's about?'

Zahira thought for a while, seemingly wondering if she could trust him. Angami could see how hesitant she was. He didn't blame her. These days you couldn't trust anyone. Least of all the authorities.

'Tanya was too tied up with the Rohingya crisis, Inspector. It was her life's work. She had been going to Cox's Bazar the past several years, volunteering and trying to get the world's attention over their plight. She had submitted several documentary interviews to the UNHCR. She was relentlessly trying for the resolution of the crisis within Myanmar and convincing neighbouring countries, including India, to provide a haven for the refugees until then. It's too much of a burden for Bangladesh to handle it alone. She was trying to put pressure on the Indian government to become a signatory to the Refugee Convention. Mohsina's interview was part of the project. Tanya was single-handedly trying to save dozens of Rohingya families who were under direct threat from the Myanmar Army or whose lives were in jeopardy in Bangladesh. Mohsina and her family came to India thanks to Tanya's efforts.'

'Tell me more about Tanya and her personal life, Zahira. Did she have enemies? Anyone who disliked her enough to kill her?'

'Not sure where to begin, Inspector,' said Zahira, tears streaming down her face. 'Tanya was someone you would never forget had you met her. It was hard to ignore her. She exuded life and was damn good at her work. I am not sure if she had enemies, but she did piss many people off with the kind of exposés she had done. Politicians, mafias and, in recent times, the Myanmar government and their lobby here.

'We had known each other since we were kids. Went to the same school and later college. We wanted to change the world, she and I, being as idealistic as we were. But she was the brave one. Last year, she won the Sigma Delta Chi award in the 'breaking news photography' category, for capturing a naked refugee child wading through the waters to reach the shore from the Naf.

'She was working on an investigative report that implicated a few high-profile ministers. It was a high-risk sting operation about the recent money laundering and sex trafficking case that has been all over the news. You would have read about it. I lost touch with her several days before she left for Kohima. She wanted it that way. She said those who were tailing her were also targeting people who were close to her.' Zahira was inconsolable by now.

'I did read about the trafficking report in the newspaper. There are many files on the pendrive. I have only looked at the Rohingya project. Didn't have time to peruse the others. I will do that on my way back. I have downloaded them from the pendrive,' said Angami.

'This pendrive has what she wanted the world to know. She told me that if something were to happen to her, the information on the PD should reach the right people. I have no clue who to trust this with.' Zahira looked uncertain.

Angami's phone rang, interrupting the melancholic air around them.

It was Dr Laxmi. She had called to let him know that the forensic report had come back with one final detail. Tanya Singh was three weeks pregnant!

The inspector went pale as he repeated, 'She was pregnant—three weeks.'

Zahira broke down. She was holding up until then, trying to keep a brave face and recollecting important anecdotes about Tanya. She couldn't do it anymore. Angami handed her a tissue, not knowing what else to say. She cried bitterly for a while until she regained composure.

'Whose child? Whose child was it, Inspector?'

'Weren't she and Aman a couple? So wouldn't Aman presumably be the father?'

'No, no. Three weeks means it was recent. Aman and Tanya never got back after they broke up.' She hesitated before divulging further, perhaps to protect her friend from scrutiny. 'Tanya had been with someone else the past few months. Kabir Wasim.'

'The actor?' The inspector was taken aback. He remembered the interrogation with Kabir. Something had been terribly off about him.

'I didn't mean to reveal this. It was their own private affair. And I don't think the world needs to know. Kabir genuinely cared about her. You know, Inspector, despite all her success professionally, her personal life was a mess. But Kabir...he was different. He understood her, you know? And now with these forensic revelations, I feel the need to tell you this, Inspector.'

'You did right, Zahira. This has far-reaching implications and may change the course of the investigation.'

'She had met Kabir at a Himalayan retreat centre a few months before she met Aman. She had no clue that he was an actor. They had kept in touch on and off and became closer after her break-up with Aman. She sounded almost happy. The heart works in mysterious ways. Aman had created a trust deficit in her. But Kabir was everything that Aman was not. Mature, grounded and focused. She seemed genuinely happy with him. Tanya finally seemed to have found some semblance of peace.'

'Yet it was Aman who was with her during the last few days. And incidentally, Kabir too had reached Camp Kismar,' interjected Angami.

Zahira looked aghast. She seemed confused about it all.

This case will be in for the long haul, Angami thought to himself. A political crime or a crime of passion? As of now, anything was possible. There was no fairness or balance to life. It was tipped in favour of chaos. Yet some of us tried to get by and do our bit to give structure to the chaos and make it bearable, he surmised.

Both of them fell silent, lost in their own thoughts. For

some reason, he could relate to Zahira. It was as if she spoke his mind. Gave meaning to his thoughts. There was a certain comfort in that feeling. Something about her was heart-rending and emotive. A certain melancholy that matched his own. Something overpowering was happening at that moment. Was it her proximity to Tanya? Was he getting involved in the case so much that he was getting emotionally attached to the victim and those she had been close to? It had happened to investigating officers before. Shadow attachment, he called it. He couldn't allow himself to be that. He would lose all sense of perspective and objectivity then.

'Any idea where Mohsina and her family may be right now, Ms Choudhary?'

'After she left for Kohima, we lost touch, Inspector. The last time she called was on the day she was killed. She seemed upset that day. She called me several times throughout the day, telling me there was something she wanted to hand over for safekeeping. She said she would give it to me once they returned from Kohima. A copy of the pendrive was with Aman, she said.'

'Did she tell you what she was worried about?'

'No, she said it was just a sixth sense. I guess Tanya was feeling the negative energies around her too intensely. She didn't want to talk about it over the phone. I think it could have been about the exposé. Ram Nair was at Camp Kismar, she told me. She feared for her life for some reason.'

'Thank you for your time, Zahira. Please do look at the files. Keep them safe. Tanya had a reason for keeping all this under wraps. She wanted you to have it. She must have known what you would want to do with it. But not until the investigations are over. Do call me if you need anything.' He handed his card to her.

'Thank you, Inspector. I will. I just need closure. Thank you so much.'

He nodded and smiled.

On his way back to the hotel, all the information Zahira had shared ran through Angami's mind. The child trafficking exposé, Tanya's tumultuous personal life, her work with the Rohingyas, the recent exposé that irked the political party and their coteries in power, the pregnancy... The more he examined the information he had gathered, the more convinced he felt that there was also a political angle to all this. The hotel where he was staying was located near India Gate. Illuminated by a thousand lights, the structure was symbolic of the sacrifices of hundreds of thousands of Indian soldiers during World War I. It overlooked Rajpath, Lutyens' Delhi, the hot seat of Indian parliamentarians where decisions of national security and governance were taken as well as political high drama happened.

From his bed, Angami could see the panoramic landscape of the city. How serene and magnificent it looked. He felt so insulated in his plush four-star hotel, far from the madding crowd. Angami thought of his future. He wanted this case to be his last, and then he would retire and do something different—something less demanding, something far from all the ignoble work. He thought about his own childhood and the demons he had had to confront. How he had borne it all: the drunkard father and the docile mother who died protecting her only child from the rage of her husband. Angami was only five then. He still remembered the blood gushing out from the gunshot wound. Her eyes were wide open as tears trickled down her face. He was still in her arms when the police came. And when he cried, he did so without a sound. He would not let them take her away. Finally, he watched them wheel her off while they took him to a social welfare home.

The father ran away. Never was caught and never seen again. Angami spent his childhood in different childcare homes until a reverend at the Church of Kohima took him under his wings and placed him in the seminary, the same place where David too grew up years later. Every night, Angami fought the shadows he assumed were of his father. Nightmares were commonplace, as were the images in his head. Yes, there was loneliness: he grew up into an introvert, married to his job. But he was grateful that his traumatic childhood had left no visible scars or telling personality disorders.

He had attachment issues and could never form lasting relationships. Women came and went. He attributed that to being too involved in work. He was far too lost now to even think of building a life with someone. Some of us are destined to be alone, he thought to himself. All the scars and darkness run deep, like rivers and oceans. Trapped in time's conundrum, the self learns to build walls, erect fortresses so that out of loneliness comes an inviolable quiet strength. When Zahira spoke about a certain emptiness in Tanya, he could immediately relate to it. Perhaps they were kindred spirits destined to never meet.

But right now, he had other more important things on his mind. Who were the probable suspects behind Tanya's murder? What was the main motive? Politics, love, or was it something entirely different? These days hit-and-run assassins were a dime a dozen. People could be knocked off if they refused to toe the line. Lives were just that dispensable.

There were several cases and murderous attempts against eminent opposition leaders, artists, writers and journalists. But no one saw a pattern nefarious enough to raise the alarm. They were considered random acts of violence.

Tanya, in essence, was a symbol of rebellion. She stood for everything that was righteous and humane. Women like her—and there were many—fought as if on fire. Fearless, they were out to get the truth. She had a severe disdain for the bigotry and systemic patriarchy that the country was steeped in. Lately, it seemed as though all hell was breaking loose. Much like an Orwellian dystopia, social media trolls online were taking control of the narrative, their voices multiplying as if by mitosis. No one had the courage to talk openly or critique those in power. It was like a secret army of informers, abusers and assassins. For some reason, Angami felt that things were much more sinister than they appeared to be.

He looked at his watch. It was 9.00 p.m. already. He had dozed off. The flight for Kohima was at 5.00 a.m. the next day. He hadn't realized how tired he was. He connected the pendrive to peruse the rest of Tanya's files. There was one titled Book of Intrigue. A detailed memoir of her inner turmoil and the sex trafficking sting operation. He felt like a voyeur for going through what was someone's most personal, intimate details. But it had to be done.

⁂

2
The Book of Intrigue

6

At night, when owls are perched
Eyes wide shut
And slivers of moon
Cast shadows through trees
We deconstruct our darkness
Like storytellers often do
Weaving inflicted scars
Into a tapestry of moroseness.
Left to our own wilderness
We were wolves, unafraid of the moon...

This is not a life journal. Nor is it one that wants to philosophize on it. Au contraire, these random notes are purely an analytical record of every grand emotion, heartache and loss, deceit and malice, that I have experienced in the course of my personal as well as professional life. I write this so that I can someday look back and connect the dots. Some of my choices in life have been imperfect. And an inner indecisiveness has always been the bane of my existence.

Aman and I met one evening at a private beach party in Fort Cochin through common friends. As clichéd as it may sound, it was as if we had known each other all our lives. It was so easy to engage with him. We didn't know where our conversations would start or end, but we talked our way through the night. At some point, we were finishing each other's sentences, often saying, 'Where were you all this time?'

We talked about our families, hopes and dreams. We talked about politics and art. He had in-depth insight into most things. After a while, we stepped out of the noisy cottage and walked towards the beach. It was a beautiful full-moon night, and the summer breeze carried with it the faint smell of seas, sands and oceans. Aman's lifestyle was very bohemian—a nomadic soul living from one moment to the next. He defied the conventional social mindset. I was in awe. For me, Aman dwelt in a world I could only dream of.

It was almost 4 a.m., the first ray of dawn painted the sky in infinite shades of faint gold and blue. He took out his camera from his sling bag and asked me to look toward the horizon and took a picture of me while we were chatting. He would not show it to me until several weeks later. Anyway, we continued talking. Then out of nowhere, his hands were on my cheeks, softly caressing me. His eyes were imploring mine. I could not figure out if the glint in his eyes was a reflection of the sun outside or the fire burning within us. But, by God, resisting him was futile. He had my mind completely wrapped up in thoughts of him. Conversation does that to people. Chemistry sizzled not between our hearts or eyes, but between our minds.

I really don't remember which one of us made the first move. The next minute, we were in a furious embrace, fervently kissing each other. He laid me down on the sand, looking at me as if he couldn't bear to avert his gaze. It was still dark outside. The enclave we had cozily nestled in was surrounded by large rocks. Soon, the tide would come in and water would fill the space. Yet, we were not in any hurry. I was lost in the miraculousness of it all. We made love until dawn. Time became irrelevant. The tide was rising fast and before we knew it, we were almost wading in water. We laughed uncontrollably as we dressed and ran to the shore.

'Death by love would have become a reality,' Aman joked.

'Thank God, we were awake,' I laughed, holding his hand as we walked back to the cottage.

Aman and I configured into each other's life in the most organic way. We were incredibly compatible—like mirror images. He was the wind in my sails. I needed his strength and placidity to calm my nerves. It was not as if Aman was without flaws. But they were inconsequential. He was a work-in-progress individual, he would often tell me. He had grown up in the coastal town of Cochin in Kerala, raised by his maternal grandmother because his parents were working in the Middle East. He talked to me about the loneliness he felt as a child. At heart, Aman was a compassionate man.

After a couple of months of dating, we thought it was time to move in together. But then familiarity brought its own set of woes. He confessed that he worked as the personal manager of a notorious minister, Ram Prasad Nair, infamous for his drug cartel, money laundering and sexcapades. I did not approve, and we argued about it endlessly. Ram Prasad Nair was like the rest of the political scums of the universe. He built his empire on the bribe he received as the Commerce Minister of State. Every project received his approval for a *price*. The highest bidder won. The workings of Indian politics are such. One would think that after attaining Independence in 1947, the country would progressively give rise to greater leaders than those who had come before. That didn't happen. Over the past several decades especially, corruption has become deeply entrenched in public life. Mr Nair, too, is a product of this culture. As a seasoned politician, he knows how to play his cards well.

We always tried to keep Aman's professional life out of our personal relationship. Sometimes he had to leave in the middle of night and travel to places he could never reveal to me. 'Confidentiality,' he would reason. It was disconcerting.

There were a lot of grey areas in his life that I was blind to or refused to question. I wanted us to work, no matter what. I no longer had the strength for another failed relationship, given that the baggage of my past was always hovering over my head. I had trust issues. They were the demons that were ingrained in my mind. Loyalty, honesty and respect mattered to me deeply. I just could not get the postmodernist impermanent relationships. How can one not dive deep?

'Is something wrong with me, Zahira?' I would ask.

'It's not you; it's them,' she would say, like a true friend.

I thought about the people I was always with. Those who never cared enough to face my demons as well as those who cared too much and couldn't cope. Aman and I were kindred spirits that way. I never questioned his lack of commitment to a long-term relationship, and he was always patient with my trust deficit. We were a match made in heaven, I would tease him. Because I wanted to make it work with him, perhaps just to prove a point to myself, I ignored most of the red flags.

When he came to Delhi, we moved into a bigger apartment. The long-distance relationship had been taking its toll on us. And when Ram Prasad Nair became an MP, it was more convenient for Aman to be based in Delhi rather than Kerala. There was this selflessness in Aman that was almost unreal. But as they say, anything that is too good to be true, usually is.

We often attract our innermost fears when trying our best to keep them at bay. That these laws of attraction would manifest themselves within just three years of our relationship, I never knew. The moment of truth came one day in the form of a WhatsApp message:

'Transfer INR 30 crore to Dubai contact ASAP. The Revenue Bureau of Investigation smells a rat.'

The message blinked on his screen as a notification. Aman had not locked his phone that day. Now, I am not the kind who would snoop around someone's phone, but this message was very unusual. It was from someone called RP. Ram Prasad obviously. I began reading the previous messages in the chat box out of curiosity. They were about wire transfers, real estate investments and some companies. I took pictures of the screen with my phone. I knew Ram Prasad Nair was into all kinds of shady dealings, but it seemed as if the rot ran quite deep. I felt very upset and prayed that Aman was not involved in any of this. I tried to broach the subject when we were driving back home.

'Aman, don't you think you need to look for something else as your career?'

'I don't have the qualifications nor the experience. You know my resume, Tanya.'

'Ram Nair will be behind bars soon. It is only a matter of time. He is into a lot of illegal dealings. Someday the press will come out with it. You are aware of it, right?'

'Nair pays me a lot more than anyone else would. I am an adult. I am aware of things. I know how to take care of myself. You forget I am a survivor. Credit me with better sense, Tanya.'

'You are the front man for all his illicit activities. I worry about your safety in the long run. I know how these things work. Which is why I am telling you.'

'I know that. But I owe him. He has bailed me out in a lot of instances, especially when I was young and reckless. Our connections go way back.'

'You don't owe him anything. It's your life. And you must reclaim it.'

'What if I don't want to? What if this is the life I wish to lead? Would you hold it against me? There's a lot you don't know about me, Tanya. And I fear that the more you become familiar with me, the more you will dislike me. I will make changes to my lifestyle and career only when I feel compelled to. And I don't appreciate anyone trying to coerce me into it.'

I stared at him a bit shocked and quite upset. This was the first time I had heard him speak this way. I desperately wanted to avoid confrontation in our relationship. But his stubborn attitude was oddly disconcerting. I didn't respond.

I wanted us to work, but was I willing to make space for someone who guarded his privacy and life so zealously? I was not sure. Aman often asked me to trust him, including his work ethic, choices and constant absences. But how was one to put faith into things one did not know about? As a photojournalist, I have been taught to trust the absolute rationality of belief based on veritable evidence. I applied the same logic to my relationships as well. Aman was asking for the impossible.

Ram Nair was a man of questionable repute. His shenanigans were well-known in media circles, though no one reported about them overtly. His political influence and underworld connections were intimidating for anyone who dared question him. India was fast turning into a land overrun by mafia culture. Governments condoned and normalized it. Ram Prasad was a political don. He won elections by virtue of money power and muscle-flexing. In the news media circles, there were rumours that his henchmen were involved in human trafficking, land grabs and illegal mining, among other illegal activities. This was an exposé waiting to happen. For a moment, I refrained myself from thinking of Aman. I hated myself for allowing personal compulsions to come in the way of my professional instincts. I had never done that. Or compromised my ethics and value system in any way. But now the truth was glaringly in my face. I could not look away.

I took a look at the screenshots once again. There were messages about the details of several bank accounts, including account-holder names. I was certain that this was about laundering via smurfing. How stupid was Ram Nair to share such information over WhatsApp messages? The only way to probe this further was to break into Aman's laptop. It was password-secured. I felt terrible about the snooping. But my intuition told me that things were a lot murkier than they looked.

I tried all possible combinations to crack the password. My name, his birthday, our favourite holiday destinations—nothing worked. I sat there staring at the screen blankly. And then an idea struck me. It was a long shot but still something.

I typed Sharanya and her birth year. She was Aman's estranged wife. He had casually spoken about his troubled marriage and pending divorce when we had first met.

Voila! I was staring at the open screen before me! I felt a deep sense of guilt as though I were betraying him. I kept reminding myself that this was for the larger good. There was too much work at hand before Aman got back home.

There were hundreds of files on his laptop. A few of them were labelled 'Accounts'. They had details of several account holders across various banks: name, account number, savings account balance, passwords, and so on. There were names of a few companies too. Angel Brokers Pvt Ltd, Mauritius, and Rudra Consultants Pvt Ltd, Panama, etc. This was like opening a Pandora's box. Serious money was being siphoned. I looked at the balance sheets, which ran into thousands of crores of rupees. My head was spinning. I couldn't make out what these figures were about. I needed the assistance of an auditor to make sense of it all. What was Aman up to? It was all just beyond my comprehension. I got a hold of my pendrive and transferred all the files onto it. Once that was done, I checked for others. The question was, where was all this money coming from?

The rest of the day was spent at the auditor's office. We went through the entire data, and he explained to me about the money trail and how it was fabricated via multiple accounts and then layered and integrated. Close to INR 1,000 crore across 100 accounts so that the illegal funds, or black money, obtained were turned into legitimate ones and placed in banks without inviting the attention of the income tax authorities. I looked at the names. There were no familiar ones. Large amounts were directed to the two offshore accounts. My head was reeling. This would be an investigative scoop that would have far-reaching consequences. Might even bring the central government down. But what I was interested in was the origin of the money trail. If Ram Prasad Nair had illicit dealings, I wanted to find out what they were and to what extent Aman was a part of all this. It hurt me immensely that he wasn't the man I thought he was. These financial records explained all his absences and silence whenever I had confronted him. I felt sorry for him now. When he reached home late that night, he seemed quite haggard. He held me close for a long time. I wondered what was wrong. Did he suspect I was on to something? I was uneasy when we made love that night. He too seemed distracted. Something was on his mind for sure.

'What is it, Aman?' I asked him, lying in his arms.

'Nothing. Why do you ask?'

'You seem a bit preoccupied. Do you want to tell me something?'

'What can I say? Except that you be patient with me. Love me for what I am. I cannot bear to have you look at me with disdain.'

Tears were streaming down his face. I felt terrible.

'I had been alone and lost most of my life, carrying on with alcohol, drugs, you name it, until Sharanya came into my life. I think I have confided in you about this earlier as well,' he began in a melancholic tone. 'She is responsible for what I am today. Sharanya is Ram Prasad Nair's niece, and I met her when I was working for him. I was always a drifter. You know that. She made me realize that life without goals was not worth living. She took care of everything, from my career planning to de-addiction programmes. In a sense, she groomed me into what I am today. We were so in sync with each other. She was the love of my life, Tanya.'

I looked intently at the mermaid tattoo on his arm. It struck me then that it was Sharanya. How amazingly beautiful she looked. I wondered about her and why he was with me now. Why do all great love stories end like this? His forlornness seemed genuine. Why was he pouring out his heart to me now? Did he still love her? I felt like an outsider.

'I owe a lot to her. I love you with a tenderness I never

had with her. I respect you and all that you do. But with Sharanya, there is a history. I can't just will her out of my life.'

'What are you trying to say, Aman?' I was blunt. My tone must have felt cold.

'We have decided to keep aside the divorce proceedings for a while. Sharanya is pregnant.'

'Oh, I see.' There was nothing else I could say. Aman and I had been together for almost a year. The math just didn't add up. My anger was simmering.

'I can explain. We were not technically together. I was still based in Cochin. It was before I moved to Delhi.'

'How is that even justifiable? What am I to you in this relationship, Aman? Where do I stand in this grand scheme of things?'

'Don't ask me questions I have no answers to, Tanya. Please. All I know is that I care about you very deeply.'

'I am not the only one, apparently.'

'I can't explain. Yes, I happen to care about both of you. Is that a crime?'

'It is if you have been misleading us both. I don't know how to make sense of all this, Aman. But look at you. With your smugness and arrogance. It would have been okay had I known. If you had told me earlier, I could have based my decision, to be or not be with you, depending on that. But no; you led me on. Shared your life with me. Carved space into my existence. And now you are telling me that your soon-to-be ex-wife is pregnant with your child? Where is the fairness in that? You lied to me, Aman. You have adopted a way of life that fits your truth. I was just another medium. Just as Sharanya or the others were.'

Aman refused to react. That was his signature trait when

he was upset. He remained distant. His expression changed from apologetic to stoic.

'Fine, if you have figured me out so well. If my love for you isn't enough to convince you, I guess I have failed. I can't change the way I am, Tanya. Not for you, nor for anyone else. Sharanya was an integral part of my life. She is carrying my child. It is hard for me to ignore that.'

'I have nothing to say then, Aman.' I was in tears. The helplessness and desperation were consuming me. That familiar sense of abandonment was churning in my chest and struggling for release. I was on my bed weeping uncontrollably.

I wasn't aware when I drifted off to sleep. When I woke up, it was past 11.00 p.m. The apartment was eerily silent except for the sound of traffic outside. I walked around only to realize that the cupboard was empty. His clothes, toiletries, books, suitcases…everything was gone. Not even a letter or message. I tried calling him on his cell. No answer. I turned to the bottle of Shiraz. My companion in melancholy. The wine helped dull my pain.

I woke up the next day with a bad hangover. I made up my mind to reclaim my life. Last night was the catharsis that my mind and body needed. I had my career and a huge responsibility towards people who relied on my journalistic work. I, a woman whose life's work was meant to change the lives of millions, could not allow a personal setback to come in the way. I imagined what my feminist friends would say. Their scorn at my vulnerability. At a frailty that negated all that I stood and fought for.

This state of limbo, of nothingness once everything went south, was not something I was emotionally equipped for. Nothing lasts forever. Relationships burn out—sometimes out of incompatibility but mostly out of in-equilibrium. There will always be someone who cared too much for someone who did not care enough. The universe, I gathered, was engineered that way.

I never expected Aman to leave as abruptly as he did. What hurt was not the leaving but the knowledge that it affected me more than it did him. Such indifference cut through like a knife. Perhaps I needed to see a counsellor, as Zahira suggested. Some impersonal perspective would help. I simply did not have the luxury of time. Everything could wait. Work was the only priority right now.

If I went ahead with the investigative story on Ram Nair, Aman would definitely think of it as revenge. He would then hate me forever for invading his privacy. Did I care? I had a conscience to answer to. Maybe all this happened for a reason. Sharanya was and will always be his priority. They were having a child. I had to be the magnanimous one and accept facts and move on. Life seemed to be a series of repetitive chapters. Each beginning and ending the exact same way. Perhaps this is what Zahira had once called *qadr*, or destiny. The preordained archetypal patterns we unintentionally follow in our lives.

◆

I went through the files again. The names and account numbers were swirling in my mind. I had to find a connection. Most of the transactions were made using accounts in Bank of India and other national banks. I had a contact at BoI who owed me a favour. I decided to pay her a visit. I told her I had a list of names and requested her to access the KYC files and give me some details of them. She was alarmed at first, but when

I told her about the possible illegal transactions that could be happening right under her nose, she complied.

'If that is the case, these could be false identities, you know. Duplicated and forged. Fraudsters currently rely on synthetic identities.'

'I realize that,' I told her. 'But out of the 100 account holders in this bank alone, there will always be a few that are authentic.'

Fifteen minutes later, she came back with the printout. I thanked her and left.

Perusing the list was a serious task in itself. Many predictable, generic names. Perhaps non-existent fake identities stitched together using real people's data and made-up data that we may never be able to trace. There were 110 of them. Scattered across New Delhi, Gurgaon and other parts of the NCR. Suddenly, I saw a name that rang a bell: Manoj Yadav. I knew the name but couldn't recall where I had heard it before. There was another one too: Malini Raj. And then it came to me: I had often overheard Aman mention these names over calls. I looked at their addresses and found that both shared the same location and address. I decided to go there and have a look.

7

Kalindi Kunj, a Rohingya refugee camp, was a good half-hour drive from home and with Delhi's traffic, it could get worse. I parked the vehicle near a garage a kilometre away from the camp. It's funny how refugee camps and slums look identical across the world. It reminded me so much of Kutupalong. Kalindi Kunj, however, was a sight to behold: it was order in chaos. Overcrowded, it had rows and rows of shelters made from pieces of wood, plastic and tin. Despite all odds, people survived and thrived there, with a roof over their family's heads and food in their bellies. Most homes were single-room dwellings. During the summers, these houses would be like furnaces due to the tin roofs, and in the monsoons, they would be flooded due to waterlogging. It was hard to imagine how people lived there, going about their daily lives and trying to make a living. The immigrants, however, were only too glad that they were relatively safe for now. The ugly truth, as in any part of the world, was that they remained susceptible to human trafficking. A battle we human rights activists fight every day.

Locating Manoj and Malini's home in Kalindi Kunj was tough. It was like trying to find a needle in a haystack. About 1,000 families stayed there in the cramped huts. The house was a few lanes away but very different from the rest that lined the camp. It looked fancy compared to the slums that made up Kalindi Kunj's landscape. This one was made of concrete, and its walls were painted in bright pink and blue. The house stuck out like a sore thumb. I rang the bell. A woman in a pale blue saree, with flowers in her hair, opened the door chewing paan. She seemed suspicious about my presence.

'Who are you?' she asked rudely.

'I am looking for Malini Raj.'

'That's me.'

'Hello, I am Sukanya. I work for Mr Aman,' I lied.

The moment she heard Aman's name, her expression changed. Almost immediately, she was courteous and invited me inside. I sat in the living room and started recording our conversation.

I could tell she was nervous. I sat there not saying a word and simply looked around. I was playing with her guilt. After a while she broke down, saying, 'Forgive me, Mem Saheb, I have no idea where the money went.'

I feigned anger, though I had no clue what she was talking about.

'You do realize that Aman Kumar does not approve of what's happened.' I was throwing stones in the dark.

'We are really sorry, Mem Saheb. If Boss comes to know, he will not spare us.' I knew she was referring to Ram Prasad Nair.

'When will you repay the amount. Where's Manoj?'

She was crying by now. 'He is on his way to Noida, madam. To collect a consignment.'

'What consignment, Malini?'

'Arre, madam, I don't know all those details. Manoj never tells me, nor do I ask. But he did mention that there was a big party happening tonight, with many important people, at Lotus Resort. There's a huge consignment to be delivered there.

Manoj has gone to collect it from his supplier. He's gone with the girls from here in Kalindi Kunj.'

'What girls?'

'Madam, those *churri* Rohingya girls.'

It wasn't drugs alone. He was trafficking immigrant women!! I knew I had to act soon. I needed to be there. I needed to gather evidence.

'Please tell Aman sir to give us one more week. It was Manoj's sister's marriage. He had to draw 20 lakh rupees from his account to pay the debt. We will deposit it back soon.' She was in tears again.

'I will let him know. Don't worry,' I assured her.

She went inside one of the rooms and handed me a packet. I examined it. A 100 g packet of a white and powdery substance. Cocaine. In Delhi, a gram of this would sell for INR 1,500 on lean days and for a whopping INR 5,000 on the weekends!

'This is the *maal* he is carrying.'

'Has Aman sir seen any of this?'

'He doesn't ask any questions about our operations, madam. Aman sir just handles the finances.'

Somehow I was relieved to hear that. I was not sure how much she knew. Everything made sense now. Ram Nair had parallel businesses presumably running operations on the dark web. It was his misfortune that I happened to intercept the text messages. The topmost priority in my mind, at the time, was to trace where the rave party was going to happen. I was very sure that Ram Nair would definitely be there. I had to collect visual and other evidence to build a strong case against the bastard.

I knew I had time only until Manoj and Malini spoke to each other. Manoj would definitely call Aman to confirm things and then it would be all out in the open.

I needed back-up. There was no way I could do this alone. I couldn't trust anyone in Delhi. Everyone was politically connected one way or the other. I thought of Kabir then. He had messaged me a few days ago to let me know that he was in Delhi for work. Maybe this was a sign. I didn't think twice. Kabir and I go a long way back. We had met briefly at the Himalayan Retreat, a yoga and meditation centre in Dharamshala, during the winter of 2016. I still remember how instantly we connected. Although Kabir was a huge star of the Hindi film industry, he was going through a slump in his career when he arrived for the retreat. But that didn't seem to bother him. He was as nonchalant about his success as he was about the lack of it. Initially, I couldn't quite recognize him. It was only after we started talking that I came to know he was Kabir, the superstar.

'Ex-superstar,' he would correct me, laughing.

Talking to Kabir was easy. He would tell me how meditation helped him deal with the highs and lows of stardom. And I would tell him about the challenges of being a female photojournalist. We were inseparable during those two weeks in Dharamshala. The magic of the sleepy town and snow-capped mountains held a special place in our hearts. And on the last day of the retreat, we travelled to the Mcleod Ganj camp. I will never forget that time as long as I live. How we talked through the night beneath the stars! When it was dawn, Kabir kissed me.

'They say that if you kiss someone at the first ray of sunlight, they are your soulmate,' he said, smiling.

'You just made that up,' I retorted, laughing nervously, unable to look away from the depths of his gaze. His eyes were grey and hypnotic.

'Stay.'

'I can't. The real world beckons me.'

We promised to keep in touch. If we were meant to be, the universe would conspire to make it happen, as Paulo Coelho once said. But life got the better of us. Kabir was busy setting up his private security company, and I was busy chasing my impossible dream of making the world a better place.

That day seemed like a lifetime ago, but every detail was still vivid in my mind. When I got his message, I smiled thinking it couldn't have been at a more opportune moment. At that point, he seemed to be the only person I could depend on. I dialled his number.

'Hello.' Kabir was smiling. I could hear it in his tone. 'So, you do remember me!'

'How could I not?'

He was right. Upon getting back, work had consumed me. There was little time to think over what had transpired in Mcleod Ganj. I felt horrible now.

'Kabir, I am sorry. I have been tied up with a hundred things. I know I should have got in touch. But right now, I need your help with an emergency. I saw your message that you are in Delhi. I can't think of anyone else I can trust.'

'And here I was thinking you were trying to avoid me,' he laughed. 'Tell me what's wrong?'

I narrated the sequence of events to him.

'And if we don't act now, we will lose the opportunity to get the evidence, and this will continue unabated. I heard from one of the account holders, Malini, that there is a very important event happening tonight. Manoj is on his way to the venue with the cocaine consignment. Not just that, he has taken Rohingya women, possibly young girls too! We need to get there, Kabir. There's little time to lose. We need to do this very carefully and strategically because I need solid evidence to implicate Ram Nair as the mastermind behind the entire operation. I want that scum behind bars.'

'Where are you now, Tanya?'

'I am in Kalindi Kunj, Kabir.'

'That's fine. Wait for me outside. Stay in your car. Don't let anyone see you.'

Kabir reached earlier than expected, in a Volvo SUV. I caught my breath seeing him walk towards me. How I had missed him. I smiled, delirious at seeing him again.

'What do you have in mind, Kabir? Who are those men?' I asked upon noticing a few men in his car.

'We need them, Tanya. If we wish to execute our plan completely.'

We got right to the point without wasting time on niceties.

'Trust me. The way I see it, you are taking on some very powerful people," he continued. 'Besides Ram Nair, I am sure there are others involved too. I have a few connections. I am simply using them. These men are part of a private investigative team. I have hired them. We can trust them to do their job. Here's the plan. We get to the Lotus Resort that you had mentioned and wait outside. We will be taking pictures and recording everything using surveillance cameras. That will be your veritable proof. Meanwhile, I have contacted the DIG and briefed him. He is a friend of mine. As soon as they arrive, we leave. There is an element of risk. There are chances that at any point in time things could go wrong. But this is what I have in mind. I hope you realize the repercussions, Tanya. I would hate to do anything that could jeopardize your safety or threaten your life.'

'I am unafraid. Kabir, You should know that by now.

I want these thugs caught on camera. Whoever they are.'

It was already 6.30 p.m. It took us half an hour to reach Lotus Resort. The alley was dark and eerily quiet. It looked like a ghost town with hardly anyone on the streets. It was hard to believe that just a few blocks away there was a bustling city.

Kabir was lost in his thoughts. He must have been wondering if we could pull this off. He did not have to do this.

'I want you to know how much this means to me, Kabir. I really do.' I had tears in my eyes.

'I'd do this even if you weren't involved, Tanya. There are such horrific incidents happening in this country these days. Men have turned into beasts. Nothing changes. It only festers.'

'In my line of work, you see such incidents on a daily basis. But I can't even begin to imagine how it must be for someone who has lived through it.' I knew where he was coming from. His traumatic childhood. Losing his parents right in front of his eyes amid the Gujarat riots. I hugged him close across the seat.

Kabir whispered something incoherently. And the next minute we were kissing, in the dark, in that uncertain moment, with only a distant lamp post lighting the derelict pavement and the sound of the air conditioner breaking the silence of our embrace. I don't remember how long we sat that way, refusing to let go of each other, until the glaring headlights of a vehicle interrupted us.

'It's them.'

'Here's the idea, Tanya. You will walk into the resort along with the girls. You will be wearing this wire with a surveillance camera. No one will notice you. There are too many of them. So just blend in. Once inside, watch out for everything. I think this will also give you an opportunity to shoot crucial pictures. Once you are done, give us a signal. The police will arrive soon. We will all be waiting for your cue.' Kabir's plan was foolproof. I was amazed at his attention to every detail. And yet I was nervous and scared. I had no clue what to expect there. I just prayed Aman wouldn't be involved in all this. Everything else, I would be able to handle.

'Take care, love, and don't do anything too adventurous. Stay low,' Kabir said.

I hugged him before stepping out.

As I looked over my shoulder, I could see Kabir's silhouette in the distance. I knew he was as worried as I was. More than a dozen well-dressed women got out. The girls were well-groomed. One could hardly tell they were from the slums of Kalindi Kunj. I wasn't surprised. I was too tired to feel shocked anymore. I went in with the group. We were hurriedly taken into the mansion. There were several guards at the entrance of the impressive black Gothic gates. I could see CCTV cameras everywhere. This place had some serious security cover. The resort must belong to someone very important and with a lot of clout, I thought. I had trepidations. I knew I would find out everything soon.

The house was very quiet; there was no one around. It had a very noir feel to it. Hindustani music was streaming from one of the halls. We were ushered into a hallway whose ornate interiors took my breath away. I could see the girls were in awe, whispering and smiling at each other.

They led us on to what seemed like a stage with a ramp. That hall was dimly lit but spotlights were illuminating the stage. We were asked to assemble and walk the ramp as and when our placard numbers were called out. It was then that I noticed that the hall was full of people. There were 30 of them—all men. They looked distinguished in their suits, kurtas and Jodhpuris. They were seated at round tables. Most had a drink in their hand and others were sniffing something—cocaine, as I gathered. It was then that I heard someone speak on the mic. Placard #1 was called out. One of the women walked onto the stage and then onto the ramp, insecure and conscious. I surveyed the audience. Drunk on lust, they were looking at her as predators would. Slowly, one by one, the faces began to register in my mind. Those that I had photographed or interviewed or seen on TV umpteen number of times. It was unbelievable. My heart sank. Cabinet ministers, media company owners, a few from the Opposition, top businessmen... They were all there. I made sure that my surveillance camera was on.

I could hear bids starting from INR 5,000, rising to INR 10,000, and going up to as high as INR 75,000. There was a loud applause. They were bidding on the women. Not that they had to, but because this was a kind of game for these men. My anger was clouding my judgement. The one who won the first bid was a veteran member of the Opposition. There was no excuse for this. The girls who were bought stood near the men. The pairs looked like fathers and daughters, some of them like grandfathers. The bid for #25 turned out to be for a little girl. She was visibly upset at the crowd and the glaring lights and was sobbing quietly. My heart went out to her. The bid began at INR 40,000 and stopped at INR 1 crore! For a 12-year-old kid. I just could not wrap my head around all this.

As much as I tried, I couldn't see who was doing the auction. He made sure he was standing in the shadows. Just then, for a moment, he came into the spotlight by accident, when the mic dropped from his hands and his hoodie fell back. It was Ram Nair! I caught him in full view. 'Kabir, you got that image?' I whispered into my mic. 'We have, Tanya. We have.'

Ram Nair was there, handing over the little girl to someone. She looked terrified, tears streaming down her face. The spotlight on her didn't make it any easier. How I wanted to hold her at that moment. I consoled myself thinking all this would be over very soon. I looked around to see if Aman was there. He wasn't. I was relieved. That's when my eyes rested on a very familiar face. The defence minister!

'Fuck, Kabir. You have no idea who is here!'

'Jesus! I don't believe this.'

By the time the bid was over, it was 10 p.m. We waited patiently. When the guests retired to their rooms, everything began moving on a war footing. There were about 150 bedrooms. Special suites were in the basement. I inferred those would be for the VVIP guests. The police would be conducting a raid in a few minutes, Kabir had informed.

There were big names in this sting. People who were at the top of the political pyramid in the country. Ram Nair was the main convener of the event. He was the main stakeholder. Other guests like Defence Minister Deepak Mishra, Opposition member Prakash Kumar, business magnate Andrew D'Souza, diplomat Mirza Sayed, and Commerce Minister Kishore Gupta were extremely powerful and well-connected. To bring them down, you needed more than proof—you needed veritable proof beyond a shadow of doubt.

Just then, there was a flurry of noise and commotion outside. People were shouting. Some of the women were screaming.

'Get out of the room, everyone! Now!' It was Kabir.

I ran out.

'Kabir, quick, there are more in the basement below.'

Kabir motioned to the officers. They barged into the rooms. A few of the girls and the men were already in various states of undress. The police swooped down and handcuffed them. The girls were covered with towels and led out. There were 20 of them. We heard what sounded like a whimper from one of the rooms. Someone was crying. It was from the restroom on that floor. The door wasn't locked. I saw Deepak Mishra trying to sodomize the child. And at that moment, I was not really sure where my strength came from. I kicked him in his hips, knocked him down on the floor and kept punching him hard on his face until he bled.

'Bastard! You are meant to look after your people. Is this why you animals get elected?'

Kabir and the other officer dragged me back. The fat man was struggling for his balance.

I let out a cry in rage and went for his face again.

'Shhh..Tanya. You don't want to draw attention. We have to leave now.' Kabir dragged me outside.

We got into the SUV and drove off.

'I hope the women will be safe. Especially that little girl.'

'They will be fine. I am worried about you.'

'I am not afraid, Kabir. I am prepared for the consequences. I will fight the system if it's the last thing I get to do.'

'I am worried about you, Tanya. All my life, I have only lost those I love.' He was tearing up.

I held his face in my palm. 'Of course I will be safe, Kabir. I am a survivor, remember? Thanks to you, I have tons of documented evidence now. They will know that soon. And as long as I stay ahead of them, nothing will happen.'

'If you think that is the right thing to do, then it's fine with me. I trust you on this. By the way, the security agency had called. They have Manoj with them. He confessed that he transports cocaine and the women, mostly refugees living in Kalindi Kunj, wherever Ram Nair asks him to. If this goes to court, he will be the primary witness.'

Manoj, we were told, had been taken to the police station, where an FIR was registered against him.

Kabir and I headed to his flat, where I could work in privacy and wire my story to the editor of *India Times*. Kabir's flat was like a digital fortress with firewalls and the works. Anywhere else, hackers or surveillance systems could tap into my system and know my location and other details. So this was the safest bet. Once the story was out in public domain, the media spotlight would be on the government. This was a mess they needed to clean up.

It was 9 p.m. by the time I finished structuring the article, along with the pictures from Lotus Resort and the pertinent details of the whole case: the bank account and network details of how the money was laundered, the source of the money trail being the trafficking of the Rohingya girls, the cocaine cartel, the party at the mansion, etc. I sent the story to my editor, Nikhil. As expected, he requested me to edit out names and blur the faces in the pictures.

'This could be tantamount to libel, Tanya.'

'They are the ones who broke the law. They should be ashamed.'

'You are a veteran at this. You know how the system works. As news media, our job is to report the story. It is up to the lawmakers and the judicial system to investigate, identify and punish the perpetrators.'

'I get that, Nikhil. You are talking like those *dalal* media houses. The buck has to stop here.'

'Tanya, I know all that. But if we don't do it the right way, this whole thing could blow up in our face. None of these guys would get convicted. We have to play it smart.'

I was very upset but agreed reluctantly. I had no other choice. I edited the final copy and removed the names.

'This is going to change the course of history, Tanya. And the upcoming elections. The defence minister! Imagine. I hope you do realize that they will hunt you down. They will try to get every dirt they have on you. And as long as you have the evidence, the pictures and video clips, your life will always be in jeopardy. You need to have an exit plan,' Nikhil warned me.

'He's right, Tanya. We need to have really powerful connections to tide over this,' Kabir said.

'Relax, Kabir. It will be okay, my love. We can't approach anyone because those involved in this exposé cut across the political spectrum. They were all in on it together.'

'How about some international organization or independent media company? What if we wire your transcripts to them?'

I thought for a while. Then it struck me. But of course. This is where all whistleblowers went to. Remember the Panama Papers?

'WikiLeaks? Brilliant idea, my love! That way, the unedited transcript will always be in the public domain to access!' Kabir grinned.

'Exactly.'

'But promise me. After all this is over, let's go away. Let's go somewhere where truth and justice exist for the most part.'

'Is there such a place, Kabir? If this country is moving

towards dark times, I need to be here. I cannot run away, my love.'

I realized we were using terms of endearment while talking to each other. I was amused and smiled to myself. Perhaps that is what living dangerously does to people.

He kissed me then. And made passionate love, as though these moments could be our last. How tender his hands were on my body. His lips exploring every inch of me. I saw a purple blue hue around us. Brilliant in its luminescence. I wasn't sure. Perhaps it was my erotic consciousness that made me see things—his unveiled soul had awakened the wild child in me.

When it was dawn, I woke up naked in his arms, his legs over mine.

'Marry me, Tanya.'

I thought I heard him wrong. I made a face, teasing him.

'Marry me. Let me be there for you.'

I hugged him tight, tears streaming down my cheeks. I was sobbing like a child.

'Shhh…don't cry. I just asked, you know. We have known each other for years. In my heart, I always knew you were the one. If you aren't comfortable, it's okay. I just want to be around you. Especially now. Be there for you, you know.'

'I know, my love. You have no idea how much I want to say yes. I really do, Kabir. But so much is going on right now. I have no idea where all this is heading. I have put everyone's safety on the line due to my actions. My family, friends, you… No one is safe. I am so confused right now. As much as I want to, I cannot answer you yet. Will you wait till all this is over?'

8

Leonard Cohen's 'A Thousand Kisses Deep' was playing in the background. Kabir was like the sky and the ocean at once—a vastness and depth that you could never really contain. Sometimes I thought I saw a kind of aura around him. I mean literally. I wasn't ready for marriage or long-term commitment. Not right now. Kabir told me that sometimes I carried the world's problems on my shoulders. I just prayed that we had a lifetime to explore each other.

Later that night, I called a couple of my reporter friends from the *New York Times* and *Le Monde* in Paris to get their opinion on my predicament. Almost all of them agreed that WikiLeaks was the foolproof plan. I decided to upload the report onto Wiki first and then break it to *India Times*. That way, the source information would be guarded. I spoke to Nikhil about the change of my plans. *India Times* would run the story after the files were published on WikiLeaks. He agreed.

I was too excited. There was so much at stake. I just prayed everything would go well. I logged on to Wikipedia and read their rules:

WikiLeaks accepts classified, censored or otherwise restricted material of political, diplomatic or ethical significance. WikiLeaks does not accept rumour, opinion or other kinds of first-hand reporting or material that is already publicly available.

Submitting confidential material to WikiLeaks is safe, easy and protected by law.

Click here to securely submit a file online (bank-grade encrypted submission, no logs kept)

Over 100,000 articles catalyzed worldwide. Every source protected. No documents censored. All legal attacks defeated.

All staff who deal with sources are accredited journalists. All submissions establish a journalist-source relationship. Online submissions are routed via Sweden and Belgium which have first-rate journalist-source shield laws. In Sweden, not only does the law provide protection against any official inquiry into journalists' sources, but it allows a source whose identity has been revealed without permission to initiate criminal prosecutions against an unfaithful journalist who has breached his or her promise of confidentiality.

WikiLeaks has released more classified intelligence documents than the rest of the world press combined.

I looked at Kabir and pressed his hands tight.

'This is it, love. This is it.' I said a little prayer in my mind. It was a 50-page transcript, with dozens of pictures. Pictures which revealed everything: the nature of crime, location, names, faces, and more.

'Money Laundering, Drugs & Refugee Sex Trafficking: India's Hall of Shame'

It all took about 1.5 hours to upload. We were routing through a wireless hotspot. Meanwhile, Kabir got a call. It was Vikram, his friend, the DIG of police. He said that there was immense pressure from the home ministry to reveal those involved in the operation at Lotus Resort. As expected, Malini and Manoj were picked up and held in prison for drug and sex trafficking. All the main accused, the ministers and industrialists, went scot-free. The girls were not minors, barring one, and soliciting prostitutes, in the eyes of the law, was not as big a crime, especially if it involved power brokers. Everything was hushed.

'This could fireball into international coverage, Kabir. A diplomatic PR disaster. It would be bad for the country's image. I told Ram Nair that I acted on a tip and had no idea who were involved. For the time being he has bought my story. It won't be long,' Vikram warned him.

Kabir was quiet for a while. 'You have done enough. I don't wish to cause you any more trouble, Vicky.'

'Just be safe, Kabir. I am with you if there is any need. Just be careful every step of the way.'

By the time the files were uploaded, it was late. It would take at least a few days before they were available in the public domain. I knew WikiLeaks had a story verification process by their own independent journalists but was unaware about their protocols in place in India. We simply had to wait.

We sat there in silence for a while, not knowing what the future held for us. But we had each other. I kept logging into my mail and the WikiLeaks website to check for any updates. Nothing. We were running out of crucial time. After a while, both Kabir and I drifted off to sleep, holding each other.

♦

'Tanya, I think you need to look at this.' Kabir woke me up with a start.

And there it was—tens of thousands of worded documents and pictures finally published on WikiLeaks.

'Oh my God, Kabir! It's finally out!' I cried with joy.

'Congratulations, my love. The battle is now almost half-won!'

'The article has been published, Nikhil,' I told my editor.

'That's great, Tanya. Make sure the Indian media gets wind of the WikiLeaks exposé. Even if a handful do, it would be enough to start a wave. It will become incumbent on the government to do a detailed investigation. Do it anonymously. Ram Nair is not leaving any stone unturned. He is totally pissed off. If this comes out, his career and that of others in the cabinet will be in the line of fire. The government will not want this hanging on their heads, with the elections coming up in a few months. They will do everything in their power to derail the news story from coming out.'

'Thanks, Nikhil. Not sure what else to say.'

'You take care and call me whatever the situation.'

Later that day, Kabir and I went to my flat to collect a few things. The front door was left open. Someone had broken into the apartment. The furniture was in disarray. The entire place was like a hurricane-hit zone. Clothes, papers, shoes, all thrown about. Couches, cushions and beds, all torn up. Everything was scattered or broken. They were probably searching for the pendrive or any semblance of evidence. I sat there agape. I was at a breaking point. Not sure of how much more I could endure.

Kabir was angry. 'Tanya, we can stop this right now. I am not sure if we are strong enough to stand against the entire system. They are an army. We are just the two of us.'

I worried for him. Upset that I had dragged him into this. He didn't deserve it. This was my battle. I had no right to involve him. I didn't say much. Our lives could really be in danger.

I could sense that Kabir was losing his courage. Not for himself but for me.

'I know, love. But this is my life. And this is how it's going to be. Fear has never stopped me. Once this is done, it's all over, my love. I promise.'

'That will be the beginning of everything, Tanya. It is going to snowball into something we will no longer be able to control.'

'This is not just any crime, Kabir. These guys are not humans. I am sure this is not the only trafficking ring that he runs. It goes a lot deeper. This is just the tip of the iceberg.'

'Leave it to the authorities, Tanya. Let them deal with it after this.'

I looked at him. My heart sank every time he spoke. I thought of what we could have had. A beautiful life—a family, that cottage up in McLeod Ganj where we first met. and my undeniable love for him. But none of that mattered. I realized that no matter what happened, my pursuit of the truth was far more meaningful to me than the sum of my desires. I had the option to give into his request. Choose a safer path. But I couldn't.

'You are right. It's time to quit. I won't pursue this further, Kabir,' I lied to him.

He heaved a sigh of relief. Inside, I was crying, but he couldn't see that.

Later in the day, I sent a detailed email from an anonymous account to share the Wiki article link with every major media house in the country. We had to just wait and watch till morning how the media would play it out. Meanwhile, Kabir arranged for us to move out into his flat until I found another place to stay. This one was no longer safe. They would come for me. To threaten and intimidate. I was no longer afraid. I was numb.

Morning light came streaming through the curtains. I could sense the rising temperature coursing into the room. I jumped out of bed and ran towards the door for the newspapers.

Nothing. Five out of six news dailies had 'The Defence Deal' as their headline. I checked the inner pages. Not even a word. My heart sank. All that risk for nothing. Perhaps Kabir was right. We were a two-person army fighting a mammoth insidious system. Tears of frustration overwhelmed me. Kabir woke up. He sat with me and held my hand.

'Be patient, strong one. Things will happen. In time.'

'I hope they do. Otherwise, what of all the work we did? What was the point?'

He switched on the TV. Nothing there either. Did I do something wrong? Maybe it wasn't a good idea to send the report details from an anonymous mail account? Perhaps it went into their spam folder? There were a million things that could have gone wrong.

I received a call just then. It was from Kohima. I dialled the number back.

'Hello.'

'Didi, this is Mohsina.' She spoke in her broken Hindi.

'Hello, Mohsina. How are you?' I hadn't talked to her in a week.

'Not so good, madam. There's a lot of trouble happening here. People have been coming around our camp and shouting at us and threatening us for no reason.'

My heart sank deeper. I had heard that there were rumours going around on social media about the Rohingyas in Kohima. That they were harbouring criminals and some such. A carefully orchestrated propaganda to evict the refugees from the region. I was hoping it would die a natural death like most rumours did. But these days, rumours on social media have taken a more vicious turn, sometimes leading to murder and mob lynching.

'Don't worry, Mohsina. I have this under control. Trust me. I will be coming there soon.'

'Thank you, ma'am.'

'Is everything okay, Tanya?' Kabir enquired.

'Not really, Kabir. I need to make a call to David Konwang. Will tell you soon.'

David and I have known each other ever since I began travelling to Kohima during the Hornbill Festival. David was also the owner of Camp Kismar, which was often where we stayed. We have had our political differences but remained good friends. I told him of the situation and requested a safe place for the girls until the trouble simmered down.

'Yes, it's a bit tense here, Tanya. People have been talking. Not good things, I am afraid.'

'Is there any way you can take them to a safe place, David? I am sorry I am putting you in a difficult position, but from where I am right now, I can't do much. Hell, I can't move from here.'

There was a long awkward pause.

'Listen, I will take Mohsina and her family from the camp and relocate them to my ancestral home in Khonoma. They will need to stay in the basement. It's in an isolated area but the neighbours can be nosy. I will make sure their food and provisions are supplied. We can bring them to the camp once you reach here.'

'I will let them know. Thank you so much, David. I will be there in a day or two. Just until then.'

'That will be fine, Tanya. You take care. Whatever it is you are doing.'

Kabir knew about Mohsina and her family. He knew how much they meant to me.

'There's trouble brewing in Kohima now, Kabir. There is every chance things will escalate. David said he will take care of them until things get settled. I need to fly out, Kabir. Asap.'

Kabir looked at me in exasperation. 'Tanya, we were supposed to fly down to Mumbai, remember? It's much safer there for us. I have all my contacts there. Plus, I have to renew my passport. In case of an emergency or threat to our lives, we need to leave the country and everything behind us, my love. You already have enough on your plate—more than you can handle. This is our only chance to build a new life together. Away from all this,' Kabir was imploring.

'There are things I need to fix before leaving. You please leave for Mumbai. Let me leave for Kohima. You can join me once your work is done.'

Kabir looked dejected. Perhaps he knew how futile it was to convince me.

⁌∞⁌

9

'Tanya, log on to Twitter. NOW!' Nikhil's message was flashing on my phone.

What I saw left me dumbfounded.

#NoCountryForWomen, with a link to WikiLeaks, was trending on Twitter. The page had 50,000 shares and 100,000 likes. And that was on the *India Times* account alone! Every news handle in the country and a few international ones were tweeting about this and the shares were going viral. There it was—the WikiLeaks article creating chaos on social media, once more. There were angry tweets from tweeters demanding the resignation of the ministers and power brokers who were involved in the sex racket. The story was breaking all trend records. This was bigger than I had imagined. No news media outlet could have had this outreach. For once, I was thankful for social media.

'You did it, my love! It's over!' Kabir lifted me in his arms. We were both laughing out loud with joy. It was one of our happiest days. I will never forget that moment. How perfect it had seemed.

We went to meet DIG Vikram at the police station. We wanted to let him know about our travel plans. We discussed at length what the ideal legal way out would be. Vikram laid out the following options:

1. I receive police protection until this whole thing settled down.
2. I hand over the original pictures and files, if any, for safekeeping. If those that were trying to intercept were under the notion that I had them, they would not give up trying to locate me no matter what the cost.
3. I stay away from Delhi for a while, until things cooled down or reached a conclusive end.

Except for the third option, I wasn't comfortable with any. Vikram and Kabir tried to convince me that this was in my best interest. But I somehow felt otherwise. Police protection? I wasn't sure. What if one of the police personnel themselves was an informer. As for the pictures and files, never. For some reason, I did not for a minute think I could trust anyone about this, especially not the police. Even if it was Vikram.

Kabir was upset that I refused police protection. 'At least until I come back, Tanya. I will be relieved knowing that you are safe.'

'I wouldn't feel safe around them, Kabir,' I whispered to him. 'Right now I trust only you. No one else.'

'I still think you should. But if you don't want it, I can't force you,' he replied, visibly annoyed.

'I love you, K,' I whispered back sheepishly.

He kissed me firmly then, trying to reassure me.

We left the office and went back to his flat. He had to get ready and leave for the airport. I was to leave for Kohima the day after. Everything was in such a hurry and there was still so much to do that we did not even have time to say a proper goodbye. The Uber came earlier than expected. Kabir had to rush down. We kissed once more, fervently holding onto each other, not wanting to let go.

The Book of Intrigue

'I will be in Kohima in a few days, Tanya,' he told me. His eyes were full. I really can't remember the last time I cried so much. How madly I loved this man.

I sat by the window. It was raining outside. I could see him getting into the car and turning to look up at me. We waved at each other. Through the rain, we saw each other as mere silhouettes. I watched until his car was out of sight. Kabir's apartment gave a sense of security. He had had sophisticated security systems installed. I felt safe here. No one knew of this place, at least for now. I tried to calm myself and think about other things.

I switched on the TV. By now, the WikiLeaks story was a national headline. I wasn't sure when I had fallen asleep. Suddenly, I heard the phone ring. I got up with a start thinking it must be Kabir.

'Hello.'

There was complete silence on the other end.

'Hello. Who is this?'

Just deep and heavy breathing.

'Speak up. Who is this?' I persisted.

'This is just a warning. We know who you are and where you are. You know what you must do.'

The line disconnected. My head was reeling. I felt faint and breathless.

I frantically tried to call Kabir. But his phone was still switched off. It had been four hours. He should have reached Mumbai by now. I could feel panic rising in my chest and coursing through my body. Fear was getting the better of me. A few hours ago, I could take on the world. Death couldn't intimidate me. I realized then how utterly vulnerable I felt that time, knowing how alone I was.

As a photojournalist, you become used to being on the front lines. Riots, wars, murders, we have seen it all. But after a while, the long-term effects start to show. Post-traumatic stress disorder or PTSD, they called it. For the first time in my life, I didn't know what to do. I sat under the table and cried. Inconsolably.

The panic attack made me dysfunctional. My entire body felt paralyzed. It was an effort to even make a call. The phone rang yet again. I cried out loud, unable to recognize my own voice. Fear was turning me into an involuntary machine. My cognitive senses were livid. The cries were not coming from the vocal cords anymore. It was from somewhere deeper, as if some inner chakra had broken open. In my head, I knew I had to get a grip on myself. I kept my head between my knees for a while. I don't know how long I sat that way, meditating and talking myself out of this harrowing hysteria.

The phone rang once more. It was a familiar number.

'Tanya?'

My heart sank. It was Aman. At 2 a.m.

'Yes.' I tried to act composed.

'Tanya, don't hang up. Listen, I called you to find out how you are. I know there's a lot of stuff going on. I heard Ram Prasad Nair talk about it. Are you okay?'

I couldn't handle it. I broke down and began crying like a child. I desperately needed someone to talk to right now.

'Baby, don't cry. Can I come over?'

'No, don't. Just talk to me. I am a mess right now.'

'Listen, I know I was terrible to you. I am sorry. But right now you can't be alone. Please let me be there.'

I didn't say anything. I could hardly think, so how could I even assess the veracity of his words? All I knew was that I was exhausted.

'Emerald Court, 26 D, Noida.'

'I am just 15 minutes away. Stay put until then.'

Aman reached half an hour later. Neither did I smile at him nor resist him when he hugged me. I broke down.

'Shhh...it's okay, baby. I am here now.' He caressed my head.

His voice. I had forgotten how it once used to be a constant source of comfort. All I could do was stare at him vacantly. He led me to the couch.

'Rest for a while.' He sat on the floor next to me as I checked my phone again. No news from Kabir. He hadn't read my messages either.

I was more composed in the morning. I wondered what Aman would think if he knew how I had used the data from his phone and laptop. How he was unknowingly complicit in the cycle of events that had unfolded. Would he consider it an act of betrayal? I felt profoundly guilty at the moment. Perhaps I should confide in him. By the time Aman woke up, I was on my laptop searching for updates from the media. No FIRs. No arrests of the involved ministers. Nothing.

'Thank you, Aman. I am not sure what I would have done had you not been there.'

'I need to know exactly what's going on, Tanya. I cannot tell you how shocked I was when I overheard Ram Nair's phone call. They will go to any lengths to retrieve the incriminating evidence you have.'

'The WikiLeaks article… That was me.'

I saw disbelief cloud his face! 'What? That was you? How? Do you have any idea what you are up against? Ram Nair is just the tip of the iceberg.'

'I know that. I just had to do what I had to do. You should know that about me by now.'

There was an awkward silence.

'We need to get away from Delhi. This place is infested with Nair's henchmen. There's no telling what they will do to you.'

'I will be leaving for Kohima tomorrow.'

'I am coming with you.'

'I am fine now, Aman. You are not responsible for me. Not anymore. I am sorry that you caught me at my most vulnerable moment last night. I had received an anonymous threatening call and had become frightened. The events of the past week have also taken their toll. And I thank you from the bottom of my heart for being there for me. But I am okay now. And we should stop pretending that the past year never happened.'

'I know where you are going with this. I don't expect anything from you, Tanya. As someone who once knew you, I just want to be there for you. As your friend. What call was this?'

'It was regarding the Wiki report, I am presuming. I guess they want me to surrender the tapes, the video, photographs, etc. Any evidence I have.'

Aman was at a loss for words. My phone rang. It was from Kabir.

'Kabir, where are you? I have been going insane not hearing from you.'

There was a pause.

'Tanya, I'm sorry but I am in the hospital right now. Nothing serious, just a fractured clavicle. I have an arm sling. I will however be under observation in the hospital for a few days.'

'What? What happened, Kabir? I am coming to Mumbai.'

'You are not doing anything of the sort. Stay there. For once please listen to me. Do not go out, nor allow anyone to come in. Not even Zahira. Tomorrow, as planned, Vikram will come to drop you to the airport.'

'You are not telling me what happened.'

'While on the way to my apartment from the airport, someone was tailing us. We sped up, trying to lose them. The driver lost control, hit the median and the car overturned. We are lucky that we are still alive. I think it was a warning. These people have us on surveillance, Tanya. We have to be very careful.'

'I am so sorry.' I started crying.

'Why are you sorry, my love? I am fine. I did not want to mention this to you. I don't want you to be worried. But I want you to be vigilant. This isn't over yet. Not by any measure.'

'Aman is here.'

'What? How the fuck? Why did you tell him where you are, Tanya? For all you know, Aman must have been sent by Ram Nair,' Kabir shouted.

I told him all that had transpired after his departure.

'I should never have left you alone during this time. But I really thought Vikram had everything covered. I sincerely hope Aman can be trusted. I am a bit jealous but my concern for you overrides my selfish feelings. Just be cautious. I will be discharged from the hospital in a day or two. Keep me posted.'

'I will, my love. You take care.'

'I will. No matter what happens, know that I love you.'

There was a sense of finality in his voice. A pessimism that was born out of an overwhelming reality that was too hard for either of us to ignore.

'Was that Kabir?' Aman asked.

'Yes.'

'I gathered this was his apartment. Lucky man.'

I smiled. I could sense Aman's sarcasm.

'Aman, this is quite uncomfortable for both of us. I am really okay now. I won't be stepping out. Vikram, Kabir's friend, who is the DIG in the area, will stop by tomorrow to drop me to the airport. Once I leave Delhi, everything should be fine.'

'Really? You think? You honestly think Ram Nair will not have his band of stooges in Kohima? I thought you were a better journalist than that, Tanya. You should know, you aren't safe anywhere until this is over. And as for Vikram. What do you know about him? You think that just because he's your boyfriend's friend, he is trustworthy by default. For your information, the conversation I overheard Ram Nair having was with Vikram. He was instructing him to get whatever it is that you have at any cost. Vikram blew your cover.'

But of course Vikram would be coerced. Who wasn't, in Delhi's administrative services? No wonder the perpetrators had precise knowledge about all our moves: where I was, my number, Kabir's departure for Mumbai, their concerted attack on him, etc. I felt terrible. I had put Kabir in harm's way. I could never live with myself if something happened to him.

'I am not here to play the knight in shining armour, Tanya. I care about you. Always have. You can't fight this alone.'

I thought for a while. There were very few people I could trust now. Aman was genuinely concerned. I could see that. But what brought on this change? I wondered what had happened between him and his wife.

As if reading my mind, he said, 'We are divorced. The papers came two weeks back.'

I was quite surprised. I wasn't expecting that. I was not even sure if I believed him.

'I couldn't live with the guilt anymore. I went back to

The Book of Intrigue

Sharanya out of a sense of duty. How could I not, knowing that she was having our child. And you wouldn't understand that. You were upset with me and lost your faith. What did I have to go on?'

'Correction, Aman. I was upset that you were still with Sharanya when you were seeing me. You had given me the impression that you had separated.'

Aman was quiet for a while. He knew he had screwed up.

'It turned out that it was a false pregnancy. The results subsequently showed negative. I felt trapped. Suffocated. I couldn't live with the hypocrisy anymore. I guess I blew it with you. The moment has passed us by, hasn't it?' He was in tears.

Exclusivity. How we all desire that in love. And yet we are all just stardust floating in space dazzling other stardusts. So, what really are the chances of absoluteness? People just outgrow each other and realize they have different paths to travel. I didn't say anything much except hold his hand.

'I just want to be there for you when you need it most. As a friend.'

I nodded. We sat there as two people who could have been so perfect together and yet couldn't. Time and circumstances had passed us by.

He eventually kissed my hand. 'Does Kabir make you happy?'

'Very much,' I smiled through my tears.

'I am so happy to hear that, Tanya. You deserved so much better than what I had to offer.'

'I loved you too, you know. I died each day you were gone. I waited. I was broken. Kabir helped me put the pieces back together.'

'I get that. I really do, Tanya. It was my fault. And I have paid the price for it.'

Aman was looking at me intently. He had beautiful eyes. Such long lashes. In them, I had once seen my whole universe and built my dreams. I lived in them. How things can change over time! There is a certain melancholy in knowing this.

I broke the sweet silence between us. 'I need to tell you something, Aman.'

'I should have done so earlier. The investigation, the trafficking exposé. Whatever I retrieved regarding the data and bank transcripts, it was by breaking into your phone and laptop.'

Aman was quiet. For a long time. I saw his expression change from hurt to sadness. He took a deep breath. I don't remember how long we sat that way, as if frozen in time. The futility of destiny, mocking us with neon signs.

'It doesn't matter now. Perhaps all this was just as well. Maybe this is my retribution. I was involved in Ram Nair's money-laundering network. I have been for a long time. I know every contact involved, where the money came from or where it was used. Trust me when I tell you, I had absolutely no clue about the human trafficking part. And when I read about it, it broke my heart. My first reaction was to reach out to you. When I overheard his conversation with Vikram, I knew that things had got out of hand.'

We talked for a long time, unaware of the passing of hours. How everything had unfolded up until now. Before we knew it, it was time to leave for Kohima.

We left for the airport at 5.00 a.m., expecting trouble on the way and trying to pre-empt it. Halfway through the highway, we noticed a black SUV following us out of nowhere. The roads were relatively deserted. The highway during this time was a hotbed for road crimes.

'Hold on, Tanya.'

The next 20 minutes were like a car chase sequence from a movie. Aman took a sharp U turn and drove in the opposite direction. As a result, the three cars chasing us crashed into each other. I heaved a sigh of relief when we were at a safe distance from them and reached the airport on time.

We slumped into the cushioned chairs at the departure gate. This could be the longest 24 hours I had experienced. Time and space had no relevance.

We didn't talk much on the flight. We were too tired. When it was time to land, I realized I was asleep on Aman's shoulders.

'Sorry.' I was embarrassed. 'David will be there at the airport. We will be going to the camp for a while, Aman. I really would have been fine. But thank you for being here.'

A feeling of dejection crossed his face. I held his hand. 'I really mean that, Aman.'

Outside, dawn was breaking. The rising sun filtered through the window, casting its golden glare on us. Reality seemed distant to us then. All we knew was the impending peril, looming large over my head—and also Aman's. The past seemed to have vanished—the loss, hurt, betrayal. All I remembered now was how he used to make me feel. Safe and at home. I was grateful and at peace. The tattoo on his arm, so beautifully written in a calligraphic script, caught my attention: 'Reality is now.' I held onto his arm tight while landing. He kissed my forehead. We were finally home.

◆

Angami closed the file. This was the last entry Tanya had made. It had been three weeks hence. Perhaps Tanya did not feel the need to record further. She really must have believed that she was safe. There seemed to be this sense of calm around her.

There were a million questions swarming in his head. Kabir and Aman, despite their closeness to Tanya, had a motive to kill her: love and jealousy. By now, Ram Nair was the prime suspect. But then again, if all these years had taught Angami something, it was to never conclude hastily. He also needed to figure out where Mohsina and her family were kept. David was probably aware of that. Angami's task would be to recreate the events following Tanya and Aman's arrival in Kohima. He needed to retrace their steps. This case was not over by a long shot. He was still clueless. The murderer was not just clever but an illusionist as well. The answers were all there, and yet for some reason, there was a thin veil hiding the obvious. Angami felt frustrated. The flight attendant announced they were about to land in Dimapur.

3
The Book of Mortality

10

Do you wonder about the smell of mortality? Of blood, soil and fauna? In the end, isn't this what we are reduced to? Flesh, blood, fascia and bones interred, decaying and mingling with the soil over time so as to bring forth life? Life is cyclical. There is no beginning nor end. From ashes to dust and dust to ashes. The trees and plants as well as the fruits that are borne by them grow on recycled souls to nourish us.

That night, too, there was a morbid fragrance in the air. Excruciating. Death had come calling unannounced. The veil of the bride was a perfect canvas, brilliantly painted in hues of crimson red, like that of Pollock's art. There was something about souls when they died young and unexpectedly—the moroseness of it all. The melancholic air was as sweet as clouds burdened with rain, waiting to fall. Death stood a silent witness to it all, as the sharpened guillotine touched the skin in one swift movement, and the jugular began emptying its crimson river.

Life ebbed away slowly, menacingly, as she struggled to hold on. Dreams, promises, the spark that held the universe, all reflected in her eyes like a kaleidoscope. For a moment, even death would have mourned her reluctance. Not yet, she pleaded, not yet...

Angami woke up startled. It was pouring outside. His head felt heavy due to not having slept enough. He made his coffee and stood outside to breathe in the smell of rain. Petrichor. How he loved the word. It reminded him of Kohima. It looked majestic during this season. Forests and mist. How he craved to get away from work.

The inspector went through everything that he had seen, heard and read in Tanya's files: the Rohingya crisis, Mohsina's story, the Khanabadosh tribe and their mythical existence, Tanya's WikiLeaks exposé and her personal life, and so on. Everything read like a movie script. There was just too much information.

Tanya, he gathered, was a woman who lived on the edge. She was the saviour archetype. Not just in her professional and philanthropic life but also in her personal one. The men she was involved with were broken in their own ways. Angami felt sorry for her, for she had given up so much not just for those who loved her but also for those who needed her: the Rohingyas, the trafficked women, as well as scores of those marginalized and displaced by riots and war. Perhaps this was Tanya's way of assuaging her own sense of insecurity. How broken we all are, Angami thought to himself. We keep searching for the same brokenness in others to make us whole. If Tanya were alive, he would have asked her out for a drink. They would have been good friends. He felt a soul connection with her. Many instances proved that. He was certain that it was this strange, paranormal connection that was guiding him through the case. He firmly believed that. If anyone heard his soliloquy, they would think he was insane. Obsessed with a dead woman. And that too the victim in his own investigation case.

He headed towards Camp Kismar after breakfast. David greeted him at the office.

'How's it going, sir? Any leads yet?'
'Nothing yet to speak of, David.'

'All of them have been restless. Unable to go back to their cities and lives.'

David was talking about the witnesses. There was a court order that directed each of them not to leave Kohima until the investigation was over.

'Mr Nair, in particular. He has been threatening us, saying it's all our fault. All this, I fear, will affect the business at the camp.'

'Tanya was a close friend, no, David? I am sure at this point in time you want the culprit caught, rather than thinking how all this would affect your business.'

David looked embarrassed. 'Of course, sir. I didn't mean it that way.'

'Is Kabir in?'

'Yes, sir. In Tent #8.'

'I would also like to know where Mohsina and her family are sheltered.'

David hesitated. 'Tanya was particular that no one should know.'

'Don't worry. You can trust me. How is the situation now, David?' Angami asked, lighting his cigarette.

'They have all been evacuated—about, 1500 of them—from the village camp to a detention centre. I know they need a place. But Kohima is in no position to relocate them. We have enough problems of our own. The Indian government will have to think of some other place.' David's voice took on a different, almost indignant, tone.

Angami took a deep puff. 'Did Tanya meet them while she was here?'

'She did. She spent most of her time with them. Sorting out travel details and other things. She said she was working with the Government of India and the UNHCR to create an atmosphere conducive for the refugees to stay in the country. For that, she said India needed to be a signatory to the UN Refugee Convention. I often argued with her about the demerits of that proposal. Especially the threat of reverse cultural appropriation.'

'How are things with you, David?'

'It's been a tough few years, Inspector. But worth it.' David smiled.

'Heard you have been active in the UNLF too? Any political aspirations?'

'Not really, sir. I am just passionate about the things I believe in.'

Angami studied David. His speech and body language had changed so much over the years. He worried about David being a part of the United Nagaland Liberation Front. It was a far-right organization with rather xenophobic views. He wondered how he had agreed to assist Tanya with the Rohingyas. But the Nagas were famous for always being there for their friends. They were loyal that way, no matter the conflict of interest.

Angami walked towards Kabir's tent. He called out to him. No one answered. He was not in. The guard who was passing by mentioned that he had stepped out into the woods just behind the camp. It was not evening as yet but it seemed quite dark there, as the thickets grew so tall that they prevented any sunlight from streaming into the forest. The distinct mountain air was sharper here—a tranquil concoction of pinecone, myrrh and ferns that grew in abundance. There was an aura of quietness, a stillness that could placate or intimidate. There were no sounds except those of a cricket or a lone monkey chattering somewhere. The mood was heavy. One could easily get caught up in the mystic aura of it all. A few yards ahead, Angami could see a soft glow, like that of a hundred glow-worms or fireflies. The stretch wasn't too long. It was usually used by village brave-hearts as a short-cut route between a Naga village and Kohima. It was rumoured that during the Battle of Kohima, during World War II, much of the Japanese artillery was kept hidden from the British in this area. There were also rumours that hundreds of Japanese soldiers were buried in this forest. No one, therefore, ventured out to these paths except those who didn't care for such legends. But they too were said to have suffered terrible delusions later.

Angami was sceptical, though curious. As soon as he reached the source of the light, the purple glow disappeared. There was nothing there. He walked behind a tree, a little apprehensive about what he would find there. His gut instinct proved right. There was something metallic on the floor. It looked like a weapon. A knife! There was a residual blue luminescence around it. Radiation of some sort. His gut instinct said that this could be the homicide weapon. Angami did not know whether to be alarmed or relieved. Was someone trying to tell him something? Was his mind playing tricks on him due to the exhaustion? He broke into a sweat. But there the knife was, partly hidden by the tumbleweeds and yet visible. It looked ornate—at least the handle was carved out of wrought iron. It looked like a dao, an archaic weapon used by the head-hunters of Nagaland. It had some kind of emblem on it. Indeed, it was an antique piece, probably from one of the stores that sold such pieces of tribal history. Tourists, especially archaeologists, photographers and antique collectors, would pay a fortune to acquire it. The dimensions fit the description in the forensic report. The front of the blade, nine inches long, seemed as if it still had faint blood stains on it. Angami took his handkerchief out and bent down to pick it up so as not to contaminate it. And then out of nowhere, he felt his ears ringing, as if his skull had cracked into a thousand pieces. He turned around but saw no one. In a few seconds, he fell unconscious on the ground. The last thing he noticed was that the knife had gone missing.

He woke up with a really bad headache. Angami looked around and saw that he was in bed in an unfamiliar aseptic room. A hospital, he realized. Kabir walked in with the doctor.

'If it wasn't for Mr Kabir, you would have been long gone, Inspector,' said the good doctor.

Angami looked at Kabir with gratitude in his eyes. 'Thank you, Mr Kabir. I had gone into the woods in search of you; someone told me that you were there.'

'I saw you lying on the ground, Inspector. I couldn't figure out how you got there. You seemed asleep but of course you were hurt. I carried you until we reached the highway and then called a cab. Looks like someone hit you with something heavy.'

'I feel like shit. Oh, I still remember… There was a knife there. The murder weapon, I am assuming.' Angami sighed, continuing, 'What were you doing there by the way, Kabir? No one ever goes there, I have heard.'

'I love the peace and tranquillity of the woods, Inspector. I go there to meditate. Somehow I feel Tanya's energy there. I am sure you know by now that we were seeing each other. There's not a single day that I don't blame myself. I shouldn't have gone back to Mumbai. She wouldn't have been with that miserable excuse for a man!' Kabir's voice was restrained and yet he couldn't control his tears.

'You mean Aman? She had no choice. If not for him, they would have got to her earlier.'

Kabir was upset at Angami's bluntness. 'I loved her, you know. We were planning to leave Delhi for good once the case closed. But my passport had expired, and I had to get that fixed. I realized she didn't want to put me in jeopardy again.' His eyes were moist. 'There was so much I wanted to tell her. Things about myself that I haven't really told anyone. No use regretting now. She's gone.'

'Don't lose heart, Kabir. How's your hand, by the way?' Angami enquired.

'It's better, though the pain is still there. I am unable to lift things. I had a difficult time carrying you with one hand.' Kabir smiled.

Angami wondered if it was the right time to tell Kabir that Tanya was pregnant.

'How was Tanya's reaction when she saw you back at the camp?'

'She was so relieved. Aman, on the other hand, was not happy. I could sense that. He still felt he was entitled to her exclusive attention. He could never accept the fact that Tanya was now with another man.'

'Another thing, Kabir. Did you see a knife around when you found me?'

'No, Inspector. What kind of knife was it?'

'I am guessing that was the murder weapon. I was examining it before someone or something hit me on the head.'

'No, Inspector. I don't recall seeing anything.'

'There was another strange incident, Kabir. I saw a luminescent blue light around the weapon. At first, I thought I was hallucinating. But when I got closer, I could see it well. It could have been coming from some fluorescent algae growing in the forest or from fireflies even. But I think I also saw it around the knife. I am not sure.'

'Well, if you must know, Inspector, there are lots of legends around this forest. As a native, I am sure you have heard of them. Soldiers who died in the Kohima War haunting the woods. Headless ghost sightings and even some tribe called the Khanabadosh. They are rumoured to give off such radiance.'

'Yes, I read about them in Tanya's files.'

'Tanya and I discussed them at great length. For most people, they are fictitious. But we believed in their existence. Mohsina and Mahmoud's miraculous story is a testament to the veracity of these rumours.'

'But there is no one who has corroborated that story, Kabir. It could very well be a figment of Mohsina's imagination. Remember she and her family have suffered extreme trauma and mental stress. The delusions could be on account of that.'

Kabir thought for a while. 'That could be a possibility. But the details shared by Mohsina about Mahmoud are too vivid. Plus, the fact that the Bangladesh Army came looking for her child when Qismet's special powers became known to everyone. Those things were real. Her sisters and neighbours vouched for that. The Khanabadosh are a very secretive sect for a reason, Inspector. They are the protectors of the planet and its people. Of everything that lives and breathes here but has no voice or power to protect itself from annihilation. They are the guardians of the universe. They did not appear out of the blue. They are humans in the purest form, selected by the universe and endowed with spiritual powers to give birth to superhumans.'

Angami listened to Kabir with rapt attention. He was

intrigued by the passion with which Kabir talked about the Khanabadosh. He seemed to know a lot.

'I am not someone who believes in the paranormal, Kabir. There is a scientific rationale behind everything,' Angami said, laughing awkwardly.

Kabir smiled and let it pass. There was no point. Angami was a man of logic and science. People believe what they want to believe. Their cognitive biases confirm what they already feel. Who was he to prove anything?

'I need to go, Inspector. Please do call if you need anything.'

'Thanks once again, Kabir. Truly appreciate what you have done for me.' He paused a bit. 'I need to tell you something.'

Kabir looked up at him, nodding. Angami hesitated a moment before he spoke.

'The post-mortem results came back a couple of days ago. Tanya was three weeks pregnant.'

If heartbreak had a face, it would've been Kabir's. He didn't speak but instead stood staring at Angami as his eyes turned red, ready to pop out. The veins around his temples were visibly pulsating now. Angami could feel the rage and sadness welling up in Kabir. He immediately regretted making the revelation. Perhaps this could have waited. Kabir had now closed his eyes and was silent for a while, trying hard to control himself.

'I never knew. We didn't know.' He was struggling for words…

Angami didn't say much. The heaviness of the air around them weighed on him. Perhaps this wasn't the right time for telling him. Loss became excruciating with the burden of truth, Angami realized. Someone once said that one can only feel loss, never measure it. It casts shadow lines, fragmenting our inner world irrevocably. Kabir was in the throes of that struggle.

'Let me know if you need anything. I can't stay any longer. I need to get to the camp.'

'Thank you, Kabir. Once the investigations are over, we must sit together and talk...'

'Sure, Inspector. You take care.'

As Kabir walked towards the door, there seemed to be a distinct indigo shadow around him. Angami rubbed his eyes, perhaps the injury to his head really had him hallucinating. It seemed so real. The reality of it all struck him then.

Angami was discharged from the hospital in the evening. A scan had been done, which revealed no serious damage or blood clots. Clearly, the person who did this had an agenda. To remove the evidence with minimum damage. But the only other person who had been present at the site of the attack was Kabir. This incriminated him, Angami thought with dismay. Perhaps he had gone to the woods to retrieve the murder weapon and possibly destroy it for good. But then why would he put himself in trouble deliberately by taking Angami to the hospital? Nothing made sense. Every possibility was an impossibility too.

◆

Angami met Aman for dinner later that night. Aman looked like a shadow of his former self. His speech as well as body language were visibly broken. He needed help. For some reason, Tanya's loss seemed to have hit him harder than anyone else. Perhaps that is what love and attachment do, Angami thought to himself. Some of us deal with loss in a more pragmatic way. But for those like Aman, attachments are like inherent weaknesses. The outside world simply ceases to be relevant. The object of their affection permeates everything else. Loss thus comes with a price. That of incapacitation and effeteness.

Aman was toying with the food, unable to eat. Twice Angami saw him gag as he was chewing.

'Are you okay, Aman?'

Aman looked up. His eyes were sunken. 'I'm okay, Inspector. I keep replaying the last few moments with her. I am unable to sleep. And if I do doze off, I am haunted by nightmares.'

'I know a psychiatrist here. Will call him and perhaps get you some medication. You did everything you could.'

'I thought the worst was over, you know. That when we left Delhi, we had left the darkness behind.' Aman was crying, unashamedly. Angami passed him a tissue.

'We were so relieved to be here in Kohima. Not that our troubles were behind us. Yet we felt safe. We had friends here who were like family. And without wasting time, she and I both got down to the business of helping out Mohsina and her family. Tanya completely forgot the trouble she was in once we reached here. She was too engrossed in sorting out the Rohingya crisis in Nagaland. That's Tanya for you, and this is what makes her feel alive.'

'Did you go with her to meet with Mohsina, Aman?'

'Yes, I did, Inspector. We went to meet them several times. I never left her alone. She was often irritated with me for that. But I was paranoid that way. Especially after what had transpired in Delhi. Activists of the far-right UNLF were extremely angry that she was protecting the immigrants and that she was pushing for a peaceful resolution and relocation of the Rohingyas. Kohima, they knew, would be an option if that were to happen. They invited her for a meeting once. It went really badly though, with one of the members almost threatening her with dire consequences. She was not the one to relent. David, being a senior member of the UNLF, intervened and sorted things out.'

'That's interesting. I did not know about this. The woman seems to have attracted trouble wherever she went.'

'Well, yeah. Nothing intimidated her.'

'I need to talk to Mohsina, Aman. Would you take me there?'

Aman hesitated. 'Tanya was extremely particular that no one except David and I should know of their whereabouts. She did not want anything to jeopardize their safety.'

'You do realize that this is essential to my investigation? I can assure you of my total cooperation and secrecy, though I am not obliged to do so.'

'I wasn't insinuating that at all, Inspector. But their safe passage was fundamental to Tanya's wishes. In many ways, it might have been her dying wish. The last we saw them was a week before Tanya's death.'

'I know, Aman. But solving Tanya's murder is also key to our goal right now.'

'Let me know when you want to leave, Inspector.'

'How about tomorrow?'

'We ought to leave early then. It's a two-hour drive up the mountains. I must warn you the roads are messed up.' Angami saw Aman attempting to smile for the first time. He continued, 'Tanya would always fall sick. Last time, she threw up in the jeep.'

For some reason, Angami felt it was best to not inform David about their trip to his ancestral home.

The ride to Khonoma, though picturesque and laden with faded cherry blossoms, was rather rough. The roads were mostly kutcha, full of potholes and unlevelled tarring. Yet the stunning sights simply took away any traveller's misgivings.

Angami and Aman stopped at a wayside shack offering green apple juice and hot momos.

'Tanya loved these mountains. She was more a Naga than a Delhi-ite. We used to come here so often for the Hornbill Festival!' recounted Aman, looking at the lush-green expanse.

'The night of the murder, or even during the days before that, did you notice anything different about her? Did anyone threaten her or did she offend anyone?'

'Well, none other than the obvious suspects who had tried their best to intimidate and hurt us in Delhi. Mr Ram Nair and his hooligans. Also, there was that altercation with the UNLF. But besides these, no, I can't think of anyone else or any other incident.'

'But then you work for Ram Nair, don't you, Aman? Also, when he arrived in Kohima, you were seen with Mr Nair.'

Aman looked hurt, almost offended, at the implication.

'It's true. I was trying to smoothen out things between Nair sir and Tanya. He was very angry. He wanted the pendrive at any cost. It had all the original documents, pictures and videos of the sting operation. Whatever Ram Nair may be, he is not a killer. He is a weasel. But I don't think he ever wanted to hurt her.'

'You really think that? Then how about the chase on the expressway in Delhi that almost killed you guys?'

'It was to scare us into submission, Inspector. But I don't think their intention was to hurt. Otherwise, they could have shot us dead. Had lots of opportunities. It's like this, Inspector. Except for Tanya, no one else knew where the pendrives were. Not even I. The night before she died, she handed over the pendrive to me. The one I gave you. It was meant for Zahira. Nair was enraged at Tanya. He knew that the story would eventually gain traction. It already had to some extent. The prosecutors would use the pendrive as evidence in court. He felt betrayed. He had helped Tanya on many occasions, especially when she needed to gain access to the who's who of the government circle while lobbying for the Refugee Act Bill. He was vengeful but not angry enough to kill her. Rather, he wanted to intimidate her. In his heart, he knew what he had done was unforgivable. And that he'd been caught red-handed. He wanted to try and reason with her when intimidation failed. Which is why he flew down to Kohima. He wanted me to mediate. I flatly refused, of course.'

Angami wondered why Aman was intent on absolving Nair. Why was the man really back in Tanya's life anyway? The inspector was sceptical about his motives. Was it love, as he claimed, or did he have an ulterior motive? Aman's loyalty to Nair was still unquestionable. Anyone in Aman's place would be out for Nair's blood after what he had tried to do. But then again, it was Aman who had handed over the most incriminating evidence: Tanya's pendrive. If Aman was working for Nair, he would have given it to his boss right away. The more Angami tried to narrow down the suspects list, the more things got elusive. There was nothing against Aman except circumstantial evidence. He had risked his career to help Tanya, who could possibly have sent Nair behind bars for good.

'Did you try convincing Tanya to give up the pendrive and forget about the whole thing?'

'I wouldn't do that, Inspector. This investigation was her life. If I had so much as even suggested the same, I would have lost her for good. I wasn't willing to risk that. Not the second time round.'

'And you and Kabir. How did you guys react to each other?' Angami was watching Aman closely.

'I was taken aback after seeing him at the camp so soon. He had been in an accident, Tanya told me. I know Tanya loved him dearly. He made her happy, she said. I realized how torn Tanya was between us. She spent a lot of time with him once he came to Kohima. I knew then that I never had a chance with her. I was happy for them. I just wanted to be around her, you know? I don't think anyone knew Tanya as well as I did.'

'She was three weeks pregnant, Aman. In all probability, it was Kabir's child.'

Aman lost control of the steering wheel abruptly. He spun around to look at Angami for a second but said nothing. He was quiet. He simply wouldn't talk after that. Tears were rolling down his stoic face.

Tanya was precious to both Kabir and Aman. They loved her fiercely. Angami wondered what Tanya really wanted. Perhaps she was torn between the two of them, as Aman had stated. Loyalty and love—how we confuse the two. In fact, it might've been her choosing one man over the other that propelled either Kabir or Aman to do the unthinkable. Crimes of passion were quite common. And sometimes, the most brutal. But both Aman and Kabir, at least on the surface, never revealed such a temperament to a profiler like Angami. Once again, he was back to the subject board in his mind.

Ram Nair.
Aman.
Kabir.

All three had strong motives. The latter two, by virtue of their intimacy with the victim. If Angami were to go by the crime of passion angle, both of them would be suspects. In such instances, the crime is committed on account of amorous rage, often leaving a trail of clues for profilers and investigators. Angami tried to correlate the crime scene, the forensic evidence Dr Laxmi had shared with him, and the details of Tanya's life he was privy to, hoping to understand what must have happened to her and why. There were a lot of gaping holes in the investigation.

They reached Khonoma earlier than expected. Despite the bad weather, visibility was okay, and Aman knew the roads well. The smell of ginseng and *khwanoria* filled the air. Mist was already descending after the rain, and it would take a while for it to clear. It would be tough for them to get back to Kohima before dark. Khonoma was as pristine as the last time Angami saw it, which was a year ago. He had promised himself he would return but never really found the time to do so. The village was a visual and spiritual treat. The air smelt different here. And the trees were so green and carried the scent of the mountains. The villagers proudly called it the first green village in the world. And it truly was.

Aman took the inspector through narrow lanes spiralling down the hillside. They reached a small house at the end of one lane. It had a grave in its garden, like most houses in Khonoma. The villagers buried their dead in their own gardens. Sometimes when there was no space, they would have to borrow a neighbour's plot or one at the village square.

'This is an abandoned house. David's uncle used to live here. He is no more and left his house to David when he died. When Tanya desperately requested a haven for Mohsina and her family, this was where he took them. David was reluctant for obvious political reasons. But as a friend, he could not refuse. They apparently came here and slipped into the house at night when the village was fast asleep. David gave strict instructions to the sisters to never venture outside the house. This place has a secret basement, which his uncle built during the Battle of Kohima to escape the Japanese. Mohsina's family stayed in the basement most of the time and he would come every week to replenish supplies.'

'That was very kind of him. Did you guys meet them here before Tanya's death?'

'Yes, we came almost every alternate day. Tanya worried about their safety. Rumours spread like wildfire around these parts. Rohingyas found anywhere are either attacked by mobs or reported to the authorities, who then take them to the detention centre. We have no clue what is happening to those in the detention camps. She was in constant touch with the UNHCR to negotiate with the Indian government. Tanya was supposed to present the project that she was working on, Mohsina's documentary, at a conclave in Geneva next month.'

Angami looked around the house. It had an eerie feel to it. Probably because of the cobwebs and dust that had settled in. Houses have a life of their own when people live there. Our existential aura is what nourishes their walls and corners and rooms, he mumbled to himself. The house looked much smaller from inside. There were several portraits hung around its walls.

'These are David's family, I am presuming,' Angami said.

'Not very sure. Didn't ask him much. But yes, I know that that is his uncle,' said Aman, pointing to the portrait of a man almost in his eighties. He had a tattooed face, almost grey from the ink. He belonged to the Konyak tribe. The most dreaded tribal warriors up until the mid-twentieth century or so. They were known for their ruthlessness and would often cut the heads of their enemies to hold on to as trophies. It was a great honour and symbol of courage and the number of heads taken indicated the power of the warrior and the tribe. They had a distinct look, shared by David's uncle. It featured colourful bead jewellery, headgear and shawls. Perhaps the most intriguing part of a head-hunter's legacy were the facial and hand tattoos that were symbolic of the number of heads taken by the warrior. Some of these men would have chains with metal heads as lockets, another indication of the number of heads. David's uncle had twelve. Even if it was a photograph, it sent chills down one's spine.

'Inspector,' Aman's voice brought Angami back to reality. 'Everything okay?'

'I am fine... That portrait... It seems so real.'

'I know, right? It was taken by Nicholas Kent. Remember the photographer you had interrogated at the camp?'

'Oh really? What a small world!'

'Yes, Kent took this picture as part of his photo documentary on the head-hunters of Nagaland. He lived here for about five years with the last of the surviving head-hunters. He was a guest at this very cottage for almost a year, David told us. Mr Kent was very intrigued by the head-hunters' history. He was so involved that he often joked that he was a head-hunter in his previous life.'

'I guess that happens. When you live with something for far too long—a belief, ideology, way of life, people—it becomes you, consumes you. No wonder Kent always walks around looking ridiculous in Naga clothes,' Angami chuckled.

The inspector tore himself away from the portrait's gaze. There was a definite negative energy looming in the house. Angami could sense it. Something about this investigation made him feel everything so intensely. It was unnerving. He followed Aman to the basement. It was pitch-dark. There was no light in there and it smelt damp. As soon as they reached the bottom of the staircase, they saw three people huddled in a corner, visibly scared. Angami took out his torch and flashed it around the room. Their clothes looked like rags, faces ashen and bodies emaciated. The youngest one, Mohsina's child, was asleep in his mother's lap.

'Aman Bhaiyya!' the women cried in unison, grateful to see him. 'We haven't eaten anything in days and are surviving on water. That too ran out last night. Please help us. We are tired, hungry and can't fight anymore.'

Angami and Aman hurried to get them out of the basement and bring them into the house.

'Don't worry. You will be fine. I am from the police. And we are here to help you.'

The little boy, Qismet, was asleep. He looked radiant, with no sign of the starvation that was visible on the others. It felt surreal. Angami felt as if he had known them forever.

'He has been sleeping for the last three days. Waking up once in a while to drink some water. It helps him stay alive,' Mohsina said. She could hardly speak further, probably due to dehydration. Angami wondered how David could've let this happen. Keeping them without food and water for over five days. He was angry and upset. Perhaps with Tanya's death, everything at the camp was in disarray. And all the witnesses had directions to not leave the premises. Perhaps David thought that Mohsina and her family would manage with whatever they had.

Aman brought in bottles of water and bread for them from the car.

'Thank you.' Mohsina tried to smile. She attempted to wake Qismet, but he was still in deep sleep. Angami took some water in his palm and splashed it onto the little boy's face. He opened his eyes. The child had such beautiful eyes, almost silver. Like mercury. Silvery yet dark. The only other person he knew who had similar eyes was Kabir. Qismet smiled and took the bottle of water and drank from it. His mother fed him and in no time, the child was running around.

'I was very worried about him. It's been five days since we ran out of food. We were wondering why David Bhaiyya never came. The basement where we have been storing the food was recently flooded with rainwater. Everything perished. We prayed someone would come. Tanya Didi was here eight days ago. At one point, we even began to wonder if something terrible had happened to them,' Mehr said.

'Aman Bhaiyya, did we say or do something wrong? Were you angry with us?' Mohsina was almost in tears. The exhaustion of the past couple of days was clearly showing.

Aman hesitated. His eyes were full. 'I am sorry. It's been a week. But we have…' His voice trailed off, barely audible. He was choking on his words.

Mohsina looked terrified. 'Something has happened! Qismet was right. He was talking in his sleep the past couple of days. He says he dreamt of Tanya Didi and she had wings and came to say goodbye. Please tell me I am wrong.'

'She's gone, Mohsina.'

The grief was palpable. The three sisters cried, beating their chests inconsolably. Their despair was more acute than everyone else's. Their hope for survival rested with Tanya.

She was their only salvation, only road to freedom. They had been so close to it but now, it all seemed impossible. Angami looked at them. Their frail bodies and sunken eyes were a testament to a life that had let them down so many times over. Statelessness will be the twenty-first century's biggest burden as genocide, wars and xenophobia are displacing people by the millions.

'Tanya is no more. We came here to talk to you about it. We don't know who did it, or how it happened. If there were any clues when she interacted with you or if she mentioned anything out of the ordinary the last time she spoke with you, you need to tell us.'

Mohsina struggled to speak. Grief-stricken, she seemed as if she would faint. Angami gave her another bottle of water.

'We knew she was in some sort of trouble. She had told us about it. But she also said that it was all behind her and that her focus now was to make sure that we were either given a life of security here, in India, or allowed a safe passage to the UK. She said she was getting the papers ready and would bring them in a week's time,' Zoya replied, seeing that her sister was in no condition to talk.

'How does it matter anymore, sahib. We have lost Didi. How does it matter if we live or die?' Mohsina was getting hysterical. Her voice was rising.

'Mohsina, there will be other ways. We will work out something. Keep your voices low. We cannot let the neighbours or the villagers know that you all are here.'

'I am sorry. We have been through worse, sahib. Our own army raped us, destroyed our lives, and killed all those we held close. What more can these villagers do? We are dead souls in tired bodies. Running from one place to another, craving acceptance. But nobody wants us. Sometimes I wonder at the purpose of it all.'

'What has happened to Didi, sahib? Could you please tell us?' asked Mehr.

'She has been murdered. Quite brutally.' Angami sighed. He did not want to make things any more graphic and scare them.

There were more sighs and tears. Qismet, now visibly worried about his mother's emotional outbursts, hugged her.

'Why are you crying, Ammi?'

It was inconceivable how Qismet had had a premonition about it all. Perhaps pure coincidence. The child seemed very bright for a three-year-old. There was surely an aura around him. He was wiping off his mother's tears. Angami felt sorry for them.

'Tanya Didi fought for us relentlessly. There are many people here who are very angry with her because of us. Once, when she visited us at the village camp, I heard two guards say vile things about her. That journalists like her should be done away with. They called her…eh…"anti-national". Or something like it. I feared for Didi's life. I prayed for her. I asked Mahmoud to always guard her like he guards us,' said Mohsina.

'Mahmoud?'

'Qismet's father,' Aman interjected.

'But isn't he in Sittwe?'

There was an awkward silence.

'He is a Khanabadosh, Inspector,' Mohsina said with pride. Angami nodded and smiled.

'You are one of those non-believers, no, Inspector?' she asked.

'Nothing like that. It's just that I have yet to meet someone from those mythical stories.'

'It's not mythical, Inspector. And Qismet is proof of that.'

'They are real, Inspector. Tanya has told me enough incidents to convince me into being a believer,' Aman said.

'We too thought that Mohsina was hallucinating whenever she spoke about Mahmoud's powers while she was pregnant, Inspector,' said Mehr. 'Our fatigued minds and battered souls never had the strength to revisit the past and confront our miraculous escape through the mountains of Mayu and the waters of the Naf that Mahmoud had facilitated. But then Qismet's birth changed everything. He is a living miracle. And the fact that the Bangladesh authorities were doing a camp search for him, from house to house, convinced us that governments too were aware of this half-human, half-spirit tribe.'

'If they are all that powerful, why don't the Khanabadosh save your people and free them from the atrocities that have continued to befall you for decades now?' Angami was adamant about making them see reason.

'This spiritual tribe is a lot like us humans, Inspector. They have their strengths and weaknesses. Sometimes, the evil people that dwell in earthly realms use powerful incantations to adversely affect the powers of the Khanabadosh. These are forces that can pose hurdles for the warriors of light in the course of their journey to deliver mankind,' Mohsina continued. 'Qismet was born for a reason. One day, he will join his father in this noble war. He will do it for Tanya Di.'

11

'All I know, Mohsina, is that I want to solve Tanya's murder case, as, I am sure, all of you want too. We can debate the merits of the Khanabadosh and their existence another time. For now, I just want you to tell me anything you can recall that might help me.'

'I am sorry, Inspector. I have told you everything I know. The exchange between the guards that night when Didi left the camp was disturbing. I overheard them saying that there were rumours that the local tribes led by the UNLF wanted to drive her away from Nagaland.'

Angami took Aman aside. 'I am not sure what we should do with these women. Should we take them back to Kohima or leave them here until the investigation is completed? There could be setbacks if I do this publicly. And at this point in the investigation, I cannot afford that.'

Aman wasn't sure if that was the inspector thinking aloud or really asking him for his opinion. 'I am not sure how safe they will be here, Inspector.'

The inspector thought for a while. 'My home is big enough to house them for a few days, at least until the dust settles. They will be safe there. But remember, this should be between just the two of us, Aman. No one else must know.'

'You have my word, Inspector.'

Angami took the women back to Kohima. Thankfully, it

was late and there was no sign of any of the villagers on the pavements. Mohsina and the others sat huddled in the car's rear, on the floor, covered with a blanket. There were security checks at certain points and Angami did not want to take a chance.

'Did the Indian authorities ever come searching for Qismet?' Angami asked.

'No. After that incident in Cox's Bazar, we were very careful about keeping him hidden. Mahmoud would give us instructions about this whenever he came to visit.'

'Mahmoud's here? In India?'

'Well, not literally. He appears on any full-moon night when I summon him. He radiates a purple glow. That's how Qismet recognizes his father.'

'I should have guessed,' said Angami, rolling his eyes. The sarcasm was lost on the women.

'So, you are telling me if you summon him tomorrow, which is incidentally a full-moon night, he will appear?' Angami smirked.

'Quite likely yes,' Mohsina replied sincerely.

PTSD, perhaps? People are known to exhibit much graver symptoms than hallucinations, Angami mumbled under his breath. Perhaps Mohsina's belief was a manifestation of that. But there were also those who believed her. Her family as well as Tanya, Aman and Kabir. Suddenly, a memory flashed before Angami's eyes—that bluish purple luminescence! When he thought he was seeing things at the hospital. The light around Kabir as he walked away towards the door was unmistakable! And before that in the forest. When he thought the fireflies were emitting a bluish glow. All this was…inexplicable. Angami felt like he was losing his mind.

'Maybe I would like to see you do it, Mohsina. You think it is possible?'

'I have never done it in the presence of others, Inspector. But I can try.'

Predictable, Angami thought to himself.

It was around 2.00 a.m. by the time they reached Kohima. The power was out and there was a storm brewing. Angami brought the group into his house. There were three bedrooms anyway and he used only one. The sisters preferred to sleep in one room. They had been together for too long. Separation was unthinkable. There was safety in proximity. There were millions like them, scattered across the continent. But how many could he help, Angami wondered.

'We do not know how we can ever repay you, Inspector. Tanya Di left us without so much as a goodbye,' Mehr broke down at his feet.

'No need for all that, Mehr. As an officer of the law, it is my duty to protect everyone.' Angami was visibly uncomfortable. There had been a continuous outpouring of emotions from all quarters for the past several weeks and he was quite unsure as to how to deal with all that. As always, try as he might, he could not remain untouched by the overpowering feelings of the victim's families and friends. He called it *occupational hazard*. Sometimes, they even treated him like God. Someone who would avenge the injustice done to them. And that was a heavy burden to shoulder. People's expectations.

Angami had a lot on his mind as he tried falling asleep. There were hardly two more days. And the investigation was far from being concluded...

Soon, Angami was lucid dreaming. Dipping into his subconscious, he was engulfed by a terrifying periwinkle hue.

There were bodies being dumped everywhere—on land, in water. Babies crying in boats that were sinking. Women screaming as their wombs were dug into by faun-like men with a half-moon behind anvil clouds. Humanity was at the edge of its existence. No one had even a semblance of hope. They were drowning in their own decadence.

Angami moved across the sea of bodies writhing in pain. One of them had a familiar face. He bent down to look at her. He felt a sense of familiar rush in his loins. She had big eyes. The colour of brandy on a sunset. Her skin was dark brown like the earth after the rains. She was calling out to him amidst the chaos. He was on top of her, feeling her breasts, trying to enter her. As he entered her, she pulled his face close and whispered something into his ear. He could not hear what she was saying.

Her voice drowned in the horrifying screams around them. He inched his ear closer to her mouth as he thrust himself inside her. 'Save me, Inspector… Save me…' she whispered, her voice choking with desire and death.

Angami woke up from the nightmare startled and sweating profusely. It was 5.00 a.m. Almost dawn. He reached out for a glass of water. Still feeling aroused thinking of that unique voice, he was quite embarrassed. Outside, the wolves were howling. The storm had passed, and the rain created pretty dew patterns on the glass window. Time has a way of unveiling even the best-concealed truths. The air in the room was damp. Angami felt suffocated. Clearly, this investigation was taking its toll not just on his body but also on his mind. He drew out his Cuban cigar. There were only three left in the box. Romeo y Julieta, his favourite brand, was a lifesaver at times like these. He took a draw and immersed himself in the sheer poetry of its flavour. A perfect roll with a smooth air passage. This one had aged well. The reason why he preferred a hand-rolled one to a machine-made one. Every time he ran out of cigars, which were usually gifts, he would depend on local beedis. He would hear his juniors sometimes joke about the state of his lungs. If he had any. They had a nickname for him: Humphrey Bogart.

It was still dark outside. Despite dawn coming on, clouds loomed after the storm. The silence was absolute. The wolves had stopped howling and not even the crickets dared to sing. From a distance, the sky looked a spectacular deep indigo, with dashes of grey interspersed in between. The pine trees made a beautiful silhouette against this backdrop. Sleep wouldn't come. Neither did he want it to. The cigar and the silence of dawn calmed his nerves. From a distance, he could see something moving across the meadow beyond the gate. At first, it didn't seem much. Just mist rising from the shadows of the night. But then the faint blue light started getting brighter. Angami rubbed his eyes. Was he in a dream within a dream? Everything seemed like an illusion. As if he was in someone else's reality. This was the second time in recent weeks that he was experiencing this. The familiar hue was inching closer in a human shape. Looking like the silhouette of a man covered in a cloak of galaxies. It was now trying to open the gate. Angami's trepidation got louder. He tried to breathe and maintain composure but that was easier said than done. Impulsively, he reached out for the revolver under his bed. He stepped outside into the corridor and moved towards the living room. The light shone just outside the door. Even through the gap under the door, it was blinding. Angami hid behind the cupboard, unable to comprehend what was going on. The doorknob turned several times before he heard a click, and it opened. In all the years of his career, never had Angami flinched even once with fear. But now, in this moment, he could feel fear in his bones. He couldn't move.

The *thing*, however, left just as it had come. Vanished into thin air. The door was left ajar. Angami opened it and went outside. The clouds were gone, and the sun was slowly breaking in. He looked everywhere for some sign of what had just transpired, but found none. The gate was left open, and it was then that something caught his eye. A plastic cover of some sort lying near the hedges in the garden. He went over to pick it up. He could not believe his eyes. It was the knife. The dao. The murder weapon. Someone had come here to leave this for him. It explained everything. But who? And why the disguise? Or was it even a disguise? Angami was not sure anymore. He went back into the house, had coffee and got ready. It was 6.00 a.m. Still a long time to go for the state forensic lab to open. Angami dialled Dr Laxmi and hoped to meet her soon, before anyone else did.

'Doctor! Hi. It's John Angami here. Sorry to bother you this early. But I was wondering if you had access to the lab right now? And if you could please meet me there?'

'Good morning, Inspector. May I ask why the urgency?'

'I will tell you once we meet, Doctor. It's a matter of confidentiality. I don't want to discuss it over a call.'

Before Angami left, he called out for Mohsina but Mehr answered. He told her that he would be leaving early and that they weren't allowed to venture out of the house at any cost. They were not to open the door for anyone nor step out.

'Keep a low profile,' he instructed.

'Thank you so much for everything,' she said in her broken English.

Her eyes were like those of a doe. Large and slanted upwards near the temples. Her dusky skin was glistening as the first rays of the morning sun fell on her cheeks. For once, Angami was speechless, as if some divine revelation was before him. The sadness in her eyes made her look so beautifully broken. She was all that he wasn't. He stood staring at her as she looked around nervously. He averted his gaze and stepped outside.

'No need for thank you's, Mehr. It's my job, as I have said a million times before.' She smiled. And at that moment, it was as if a thousand suns shone outside the window.

◆

Angami waited outside the forensic lab. It was just 7.00 a.m. He felt bad for waking Dr Laxmi from her sleep this early, but it was a race against time. Dr Laxmi was the only person he could trust at this point.

She came in after a while.

'I am really curious, Inspector. It seems you have had a breakthrough of some sort?'

'I think we have the murder weapon, Doctor.'

'What? How?'

'Let's go inside. I will explain. What time does the other staff arrive?'

'It will be 10.00 a.m. by the time they do. We have just enough time.'

Entry into the highly digitalized state-of-the-art forensic lab involved three rounds of access ID: face, iris and fingerprint. It was next to impossible for outsiders to get inside.

'This lab is Kohima's crowning glory, Inspector. It's surprising how Delhi decided to construct the forensic HQ here.'

'Probably to negate the neta influence, Doctor. Which is just as well considering how much they have infiltrated the CBI already.'

When they were inside, Angami pulled out a plastic bag from his backpack. He put on gloves and took out the ornate knife.

'It's so beautiful.'

'Sharp as well.'

Dr Laxmi examined the knife. She scraped off the dried blood from the knife for DNA sampling.

'I don't see any fingerprints. The murderer would have definitely used gloves. Which means this was premeditated. I have collected the blood stains. Hopefully, we should find skin cells or hair fibres or some such thing. With state-of-the-art rapid analysis, we could get the results in no time, Inspector.'

'I will wait here, Doctor. I cannot leave the evidence unguarded. This is crucial.'

Angami waited patiently, lost in thought. He still could not believe what had happened. He wondered who it was in the blue shadows. Could it really have been a Khanabadosh? It was said that they dwelt in places that had an affinity towards the supernatural and occult practices. Nagaland, that way, was the heartland of such medieval activities. Or it had once been so. Angami remembered the legends and stories he used to hear as a child. That Nagaland was so steeped in mysticism that spirits roamed free here. Each tribe had shamans who could actually communicate with the netherworld. Angami could not believe that he, a die-hard rationalist, was veering towards superstition and hearsay. Whoever it was, how did they get hold of the knife and why did they bring it to him? Who was trying to help him?

The inspector dialled home to find out how Mohsina and the others were doing.

'Hello,' it was Mehr again. Angami remembered her face looking so innocent earlier that morning. She resembled the woman in that effusive dream. Perhaps it was her. He couldn't tell. The eyes, fearful and alluring, pleading with him. He was drawn to her but felt ashamed of his feelings and brushed them aside.

It was unthinkable what these women had gone through. He wondered how long it would take for them to heal fully. If they would ever find a permanent place to call their own. Or were they doomed to be persecuted all their lives, running for cover from one country to another? For now, Angami wanted nothing more than to help them out of Nagaland.

'Mehr?'

'Ji, sir.'

'Did you all have breakfast? Is Qismet fine?'

'Ji, sir. We are all fine. Thank you.' She paused for a moment. 'Have you eaten?'

There was sincere concern in her voice. No one had spoken to Angami in that way for a long time. Her voice rang like a sweet whisper in his ear. He felt an overwhelming need to protect her. This was strange. Stirrings of the saviour complex, eh? He wasn't sure.

'I had coffee, yes. At work now. I may come home late. Make sure none of you venture out or open the door for anyone.'

'We won't, sir. I have made sure the curtains are drawn too.'

'Okay, that's good. So, see you tonight.'

'You take care too, sir,' she said in a hesitant tone.

Angami smiled. 'I will.'

It was 9.00 a.m. The office would be streaming with people in no time. Angami went into the analysis room.

Dr Laxmi seemed optimistic. 'Just a while more, Inspector. We are almost there.'

'This fast, Doctor? I was worried if it would take longer. I did not want anyone to get even the slightest idea of what we are doing here.'

'Yes, Inspector. There's a reason why the government has invested so much in this facility in Kohima. The state-of-the-art rapid analysis tools and machines and data storage devices make this HQ one of the most sought-after criminal data facilities in probably the entire world. The government is now able to fast-track investigations pertaining to terrorism as well as civil crimes. It's made life easier for investigating agencies. This place is rivalled only by the CIA's facility in the US and that of Mossad in Jerusalem.'

'Wow. Never thought our government would wake up one day and realize the urgency of this,' exclaimed Angami, truly surprised. This indulgence was long overdue in a country where criminal convictions had dipped miserably to 38.5 per cent in 2014. Criminals were out there roaming free due to a lack of evidence as well as delays in the judicial process and investigations. The new facility would solve at least a part of the problem.

'But as of now, we get more CBI and RAW investigation requests than regular ones. I was surprised that the photojournalist's murder was assigned to our facility.'

'Perhaps because of the facility's proximity to the crime scene.'

'Yes, perhaps. We are using DNA profiling here, Inspector. After we have ascertained the blood, fibre and skin cell samples that we recovered from the knife, we can match them with those we found at the crime scene. This will help us ascertain if the knife was indeed the weapon used on the victim. It will also let us know if anything on it corresponds with other samples picked up from the scene of the crime. And once we zero in on that, I would request DNA samples from the suspects you have for the case. You do have your suspects, don't you?'

'I do. Nothing conclusive. Purely based on possible motives and circumstantial evidence. But I will need stronger evidence to zero in on the main suspect and issue an arrest warrant. I am hoping the forensic analysis will help me with that.'

'May I ask who these suspects are?'

'There are three prime ones, as I mentioned the other day, Doctor. There is the ex-boyfriend who was with the victim around the time of the crime. Tanya was working on a high-profile case involving top cabinet ministers and other important people. Then there is the current boyfriend, who was also in Kohima at the time. He is a mystery in himself. There is something about him that is quite intriguing but unexplainable. Call it an investigator's sixth sense. I somehow feel he knows more than he lets on. Crime of passion? It could be anything.'

Angami continued, 'Then there's the very obvious Ram Nair. The chief accused in the trafficking scandal, he has a very strong motive. Tanya has single-handedly exposed his alleged money laundering and drug and women trafficking activities. This has literally put his political career at stake. Once the courts get their hands on the video evidence, his career will be over, and he would probably have to spend years languishing in jail. Then there are a few others too but not of much consequence. The camp owner, a photographer, and of course the guard who saw the body and raised the alarm. There is also a political angle to this. Those aligned with the UNLF wanted Tanya gone from Kohima at any cost. They were extremely upset that she was aiding the Rohingyas in seeking legal refugee status in India, particularly Kohima.'

'Sounds like the usual whodunnit murder mystery, no, Inspector?' Dr Laxmi teased him. 'But as I keep saying, sometimes the ones we least suspect turn out to be the culprit. Forensic crime data analytics has often proven that. By the way, what makes you discount the possibility that it could be someone wholly unrelated, say, a copycat psychopath?'

'There's strict security at the camp. No one comes in or leaves without signing the visitors' log at the gate. These six people were the only ones at the camp when the incident happened. I am, however, keeping all my options open, Doctor. I don't want to assume anything until I have irrefutable evidence. In my several years of service at the agency, I haven't come across a case as elusive or intriguing as this one.'

Out of sheer curiosity, Angami broached a different subject as Dr Laxmi switched slides and samples under a high-powered UV microscope of some sort.

'Doctor, have you ever encountered anything unusual at the lab during your stint here? I mean, for DNA analysis...'

'As in, Inspector?'

'I do not want to seem out of my head here. But I have heard about strange events in the past couple of weeks and actually witnessed some too, as much as I hate to admit it. Have you heard of the Khanabadosh?'

Dr Laxmi stopped working with the microscope and looked up at him. He couldn't read her. She seemed alarmed. A bit uneasy.

'By the look on your face, it seems as if you have, Doctor.'

'Who hasn't? There are stories of them everywhere. In books, movies and even the news media sometimes. Most people think they are wonderful fiction. A proof of people's colourful imagination. Like aliens or UFOs.'

'What do you think? Did you have any unusual cases that could have led you to believe otherwise?'

Dr Laxmi was quiet for a bit. Angami worried if he had interrupted her work. It was already getting late. Perhaps they should have this conversation another day.

'We did once but were made to swear to secrecy. This was a couple of years ago. I'm not even sure I should be telling you this, Inspector. It was a classified, highly-confidential incident. But if this helps you in any way in the ongoing investigation, I should tell you.'

'I am not sure at this point, Doctor, but yes, there is a strangeness about this case beyond anything that I have ever encountered.'

'There was this case being investigated by the CBI—the assassination of a high-profile politician. Amarnath Singh.'

'Yes, the name sounds very familiar. He was named as one of the accused in the Mirchpur violence against Dalits in Haryana, right? 2011?'

'That's right. As with most riots, dozens were killed, women were raped in Mirchpur village, and many houses were set on fire. I still remember media images. FIRs were filed against several people. Amarnath Singh was one of them. But as with most cases involving people in power, Singh was let off scot-free due to a lack of evidence. Three out of the five eyewitnesses went off-script and one of them died mysteriously. Six months or so after Singh was acquitted, he was killed one night. Hacked to death with an axe in fact, while he was on his way back home on his motorcycle. I was a senior intern at the Delhi Forensic Lab, the CBI headquarters at the time. It was a gruesome sight. The body had been literally chopped off into pieces. While doing the DNA analysis of the blood sample we found on the victim's body and the murder weapon, something really strange happened. Besides the B+ blood of the victim, another blood group was detected. It just didn't make sense. The DNA helix was in quadruple, unlike the double helix in humans. At that time, we thought it was some error in the machine or perhaps a contaminated sample.'

'But repeated tests revealed the same thing,' added Dr Laxmi. 'The same two samples we got from the axe as well. One of Amarnath Singh and the other of God knows what. Somehow, during the altercation, the killer had got injured too, and their blood spurted on the victim and the weapon. Further research was done on the sample, and it revealed strange findings. To begin with, it wasn't a human DNA helix. A mutant of some sort. Because it showed very similar characteristics and common components. Like the amino acid sequences and the helix pattern were the same. The only difference was that instead of double, this one was quadruple. We shared the data with the CIA as well as the KGB and Mossad to find some semblance of an explanation. Much to our surprise, several hundred such DNA patterns had been recorded around the world, sourced from various scenes of crime, terrorism and other nefarious activities. And the majority of these crimes had been committed against state machineries or people in power who were involved in blatant acts of injustice against humanity. In many ways, the DNA seemed to belong to a half-human Robin Hood sect of sorts, who were protecting the weakest of the weakest link in the human chain. This left us at a dead end because no one knew what form or shape these beings took. The Centre for Advanced Human Genetics, California, in fact, did an interesting reconstruction study using the available DNA helix. They came to some profound findings. This, however, was not revealed to the general public for fear of aggression towards human populations with similar physical characteristics.'

'And what are the real characteristics, physical and otherwise, of this half-human sect, Doctor?'

'These beings are supposed to be of superior intellect and equipped with extrasensory perception. Very sensitive. Physically, they are likely tall and athletic, with Mediterranean features. Their most striking characteristic is silver-grey eyes. You can't really tell them apart from humans except that they leave behind a bluish-purple residue, almost like stardust, when in a state of excitement or stirred by emotions. They each also seem to have the strength of five humans put together and several other extraordinary powers that we haven't still ascertained. But one thing is certain: no one has ever captured these beings. My belief is that the more evolved of them can appear and disappear at will. Their skill levels depend on how well-trained they are. Which makes them elusive and almost holographic. I can assure you that whatever findings we have, they concur with the legends that we hear of the Khanabadosh tribe! I know it's terrible for a scientist to say such things. But even the most conclusive data points towards that.'

'A bluish-purple hue,' Angami repeated before falling speechless for a while. 'Doctor, would you believe me if I told you that there was an apparition, or something like it, around my house early this morning, around 4.00 a.m., that placed the knife, the very evidence, at my doorstep? I saw it with my own eyes. And it was not a hallucination.'

'I don't find it hard to believe at all, Inspector,' replied Dr Laxmi, her hands shivering a little.

The case was spiralling into something bigger than Angami had originally conceived. Why was a so-called Khanabadosh interested in helping him? Was it because Tanya had been fighting for the same humanitarian causes as them? He left the HQ as soon as people started trickling in. It would take a few more hours for Dr Laxmi to complete the analysis and compare it with the central database of known convicts and accused individuals. The government maintained a recorded DNA database of five crore people, which was a great boon to investigating agencies. Getting a reference sample from the suspects, however, might prove tricky as Angami inched closer to the truth. In most cases, they were non-compliant.

Angami left for the camp and hoped to catch Nicholas Kent and Ram Nair once more to question them. The next couple of hours were crucial.

♦

The camp looked deserted, as most of the tourists had left after Tanya's murder. The presence of the police at the site didn't make it any easier to retain the festive vibe. A few superstitious people claimed that the spirit of one so brutally murdered would always haunt the place. There were rumours that the screams of a woman were heard in the middle of the night. David was visibly frustrated. He claimed that this was mere gossip spread by rival hoteliers. It affected his business adversely. Tanya's death loomed large at the camp. It's hard to believe that a week had gone by since its occurrence.

'Hey, Inspector. How's it going? My visa will expire in a week. I really do hope I can leave before that.' It was Nicholas Kent, the photographer.

'Sure, you can, sir. A few more days and we will be ready to wrap up. Actually, not even that long. Can we grab some tea at the canteen? I wanted to speak to you.'

'Sure, Inspector.'

The canteen too looked deserted. Angami wondered if it was functioning at all. There was no one there.

'Looks like we will have to make our own tea,' he joked.

'No. These guys must be around somewhere. Since there are not that many guests, they tend to laze around...' Kent called out for someone named Suri.

Suri was the head chef at the camp. He was only 25. He had been working with David ever since he was a 13-year-old child. He had a natural flair for cooking. He was David's man Friday. He multitasked at the camp, from being head chef to plumber, electrician, waiter and manager, if need be.

'David is lucky,' Kent said. 'His steaks are legendary. It's the way he carves them. Like an artist. I used to think Denmark had the best steaks. But Suri is a genius. He knows his meat.' Kent smiled.

Suri came towards them. He had a deadpan face, with absolutely no expression even while talking. His eyes were fixed and always had that faraway gaze. For some reason, Angami felt uncomfortable in his presence.

'Suri, could you bring two cups of *adrak* chai?'

The young chap nodded, looking at Angami as he left.

'I don't trust Suri with my tea. I don't think he likes me.'

Kent laughed out loud. 'Don't mind him, Inspector. It's just his personality. He's a good guy. I have been seeing him ever since I started coming to Kohima.'

'I understand,' Angami said, smiling. 'Mr Kent, tell me more about your time spent with David's uncle. He was photographed by you, if I recall correctly, for your feature on the head-hunters of Nagaland.'

'You can call me Nick, by the way. Oh yes. King Chingkho Konwang. He was my muse and spiritual guide. When he died, it was as if I had lost a father. I spent three years there, at their home in Khonoma village. It was one of the most spiritual experiences of my life. I learnt so much from him. He is the reason why I don't find any reason to go back to Denmark. I feel so at home here. So, every year, I renew my visa and stay back in Kohima. You are blessed to be a part of this heritage, Inspector. To belong to something so deeply spiritual.'

'So I have heard, Nick. Sometimes people and places do that to you. I was born here, lived here most of my life, and yet feel no connection with the traditions. Perhaps it is the familiarity of it all. I love Kohima with all my heart, mind you. Am just not married to its traditions, I guess. Perhaps I am too much a man of science and facts. Logic and reason are my tools for survival. Not past rituals.'

'Perhaps it is the reason why you are so good at what you do, John. To slay the world's demons. And I must say you are doing an amazing job. How is the latest investigation progressing? As much as I hate leaving Kohima, I need to get back to Denmark before my visa expires. It's just too much hassle otherwise, you know. I need to go soon.'

'Some cases take time. Especially homicide investigations.

The murderer this time is a clever one. He left no trail.'

'And yet you found the knife.'

Angami paused a while, a bit taken aback. 'Divine intervention, really.'

'How may I help you, Inspector. Am I a suspect too?'

'As of now, no one's a suspect, Nick. All are secondary witnesses. Tell me more about the time you spent at David's uncle's place.'

Angami watched as Kent lit a cigarette and took a long drag. He offered one to Angami. He was left-handed, Angami noticed. No wonder he was such a genius.

'This was more than five years ago. A few of my photographer friends had told me about the Hornbill Festival. I was fascinated with the pictures they were taking of the various tribes and their cultural traditions. Truly a photographer's delight. What got me hooked were pictures of octogenarian men with beautiful clothes and tattoos on their faces. I was intrigued and that's how I first came to Nagaland, in 2013. I was staying here at Camp Kismar. Not knowing where to begin, I started discussing my project with David, and that's when he told me about his uncle. A Konyak warrior and head-hunter in his day, he was a storyteller and taught the basic ancient arts of a head-hunter warrior to those who were curious about their ancestry. For me, this was serendipity. Everything happens for a reason. I packed my bags and left for Khonoma the next day.'

He continued, 'Sensi, as I liked to call him, was a man with kind eyes and an affable smile. It was hard to imagine how he could have been one of the fiercest head-hunters during those days. At the time of my project, he was eighty-one years old—frail yet very muscular. His tattoos were intricate and telling. His total headcount, he claimed, was twelve. That's a whole lot of heads!' Kent laughed, adding, 'I could imagine him slaying rival tribes with his sword and taking their heads back to his village as trophies. He would tell us how the heads were proudly displayed on the walls and doorways of his house. Can you imagine that? Sometimes I shuddered thinking of the kind of energy that was in that house. The skulls were still there as decorative pieces, hung casually as one would a chandelier or a plant. After a while, I got used to the bones as an integral part of the house.'

'I spent my entire time with him,' continued Kent. 'Sometimes we went into the nearby forest, where he would narrate, in great detail, the exact places where various fights or wars between the tribes took place. He was upset when the Indian government put a ban on this tradition in the sixties. That was the end of the Konyak way of life. He sounded almost nostalgic, resentful even. Once, he took me to Mon district, which shared borders with Myanmar, with dozens of former warriors still living there. We stayed there for six months. That's where I took plenty of photographs of the head-hunters with their beautifully tattooed faces and chests, large ear piercings, and war hats made of pig horns, goat tails and hornbill feathers. It was fascinating was to watch them. Even more fascinating was to see them enact and narrate stories of their bygone combats with war dances and guns and knives. Some of them still carried their beautifully carved ornate knives.'

Angami interrupted him. He took out his phone and showed Kent a picture. 'Did it look anything like this?'

Nick looked at it closely for a while. 'Yes. That's a perfect prototype.'

'It's not a prototype, Nick. That's the murder weapon.'

'Oh man. What are you suggesting, Inspector? That a

Konyak warrior could be the killer?'

'I am not saying anything. But the murder weapon certainly belongs to one of the tribes.'

'I am not sure if any of them would commit such a thing, Inspector. They have a very strong sense of honour. Head-hunting was practised only on enemies and rival tribes, and never on women.'

'True. But who knows? The definition of an enemy changes with time. The question is, who is the enemy today?'

'Anyone who threatens their sense of honour and territorial integrity.'

'Exactly.'

'But what did Tanya ever do to them? As far as I have read in the news, since her murder she has been at the centre of a storm. Some sort of political exposé. Isn't that the angle you should be focusing on?' Kent's tone was reproachful, intimidating even.

'I am not leaving any angle unexplored, Mr Kent. In my line of work, you learn to discern the least threatening motive. In Tanya's case, there are just too many. Anyway, tell me more about your story with Sensi.'

'I spent two years with him. It was an isolated life, but I loved it. Besides working on my project, I learnt how to make and draw the head-hunter's tattoos. Learnt other things too, like their art of burial, sacred rituals and war dances and cries. It all affected me deeply. I began to think of myself as a Konyak. Once, during a sort of hypnosis-like therapy with Sensi, I was singing the war cry and speaking in the Konyak language. Everyone was mortified. I had just experienced an episode of past-life regression. I was a head-hunting Konyak warrior! Sensi and the other elders welcomed me into their tribe. I cannot explain to you what that felt like. You may not even understand. Nagaland has become home for me and its people, mine. I can't imagine living anywhere else.'

'Tell me more about the village of Mo, Kent.'

'As I mentioned before, I spent a considerable amount of time in Mo with Sensi. That was also where I met Suri for the first time. He was the grandson of one of the headhunters and Sensi had taken him under his wing. He was very good at cooking. Especially hunting, fleecing and barbecuing. That was his forte. Sensi used to tell us that hunted meat always tasted better. And I must say he was so right. Every time there was a festival in Mo, Suri was always the head chef. He was marvellous at it. I guess hunting ran in their genes. Suri stayed on with Sensi until his death, which was a few months after my photo journal was published. Ever since then, he has been with David and doing very well for himself at the camp.'

Angami was trying to make sense of everything that Kent had been telling him. This looked like a blind spot that he had completely missed.

'What about David? Did he ever visit Mo?'

'Oh yes. As you know, David grew up in the church. He wanted to become a parishioner until he realized that his Konyak genes were so much more dominant. He would visit Sensi during vacations. He was one of the very few of his generation who had learnt the Konyak way of life. Sensi had that gift. To inspire pride for their culture and heritage in everyone. David, Suri and I were a team. We often hunted wild animals together and Suri and David would teach me how to fleece and barbecue. After a while, I became better than them,' Kent laughed. There was this gleam in his eyes when he talked. He was no longer a Dane by any measure.

'So you guys were the Konyak A Team?' Angami teased. 'While in Mo, how was their attitude towards the influx of the Rohingyas along the border?'

'Oh, they were very angry. And I don't blame them. The missionaries had already converted most of the tribes, and now with the Rohingyas, the Nagas feared that cross-cultural marriages would happen over time and dilute their heritage. Cultural appropriation would also be an issue. The headhunters are extremely territorial in nature. It's a tribal trait, I guess. So, when there was an influx of refugees along the border during the Rohingya crisis of the 1980s, there was a huge backlash. The head-hunter community refused to allow them to settle in Mo and instead chased them away to other places. Being compliant with and hospitable to outsiders has been followed by the destruction of too many indigenous cultures around the world, you know.

'Sensi and I used to talk at length about this. He was convinced that the immigrants were people who were fleeing for their lives. They had no other option. They were not a threat. But my thoughts were always from a socio-cultural perspective. I found it difficult to think what would happen if the culture and heritage of Nagaland were diluted. Emigration usually does that to countries, you know. It would certainly be the death of Naga tribal culture as we knew it. Despite Sensi being my guru and all, my views differed from his at times.'

Nick's eyes were red and the veins around his temples were throbbing. Only his calm voice kept the conversation going. Angami was surprised to see the kind of passion and nationalism Nick had for the region. It was inconceivable that it existed in a foreigner.

'It's too historically, politically complex to explain, Kent.' Angami looked burdened with the weight of his own thoughts. He got up to leave. 'Thank you so much for your time.'

'I hope whatever I have told you helps you in some way.'

'Oh, you have no idea!' Angami retorted.

12

David was not in office that evening. Angami wanted to talk to him, but it was already late. For some reason, his thoughts veered towards Mohsina and the others. Something at that moment made him uncomfortable. It was a gut instinct. He called home to check in on them.

'Hello.'

'Hello, Mohsina. This is John Angami here.'

'Yes, Inspector-ji.'

'I just called to find out how you are doing. I will be home late tonight. So please don't wait for me. You can go to bed right after dinner. I have a spare key.'

'We are all fine. Thank you so much.'

Angami smiled. 'Glad to hear. Take care.'

He immediately hung up, as there was another call waiting. It was Dr Laxmi.

'Doctor, what do you have for me?'

'The sample analyses are in, Inspector. That is indeed the murder weapon. The blood sample matched with Tanya's. There was however, as we suspected earlier, another blood type on the knife. I ran a comparative analysis using the available database. There was no match. So this person isn't a convicted criminal. Yet. Also, I wanted to tell you something. The knife itself is a hundred years old. It's made of carbon steel, the kind which swords are usually made of. Its purpose was to be used as a weapon. Definitely not a decorative piece or a kitchen item. I looked up the intricate designs on the knife, Inspector. It is indeed a dao, a Konyak weapon belonging to the head-hunters.'

'That's invaluable information, Doctor. Thank you. Anything else? Were there any fingerprints?'

'No, nothing. The killer strangled her first and when she almost lost consciousness, he decapitated her. Not sure how the killer's blood got on the knife though. I am guessing he panicked a bit while the victim struggled when he slit her throat. The incision was precise. This knife is so sharp and powerful that it cut the throat in the first go. I am guessing it was sharpened rather recently. Else, considering how old it is, the knife should have been quite blunt now. This kind of incision would not have been possible without it being sharpened recently.'

Angami looked around. It was as if something came to him in a flash. It was there and yet it wasn't. He remembered seeing something distinctly clear. Wasn't it an antique knife sharpener? He just couldn't be sure. 'Think, think,' he told himself. But his mind was foggy, and some things were just not adding up. And then out of the blue, like an epiphany, it all dawned on him. He needed to get *there* ASAP.

◆

From a distance, it looked as if they were having a friendly chat. Two alpha males who had just lost the woman they loved. They were outside Kabir's tent. Their voices were growing louder. On closer inspection, it turned out to be an altercation. Angami rushed, hoping to stop them from coming to blows.

'You son of a bitch! I know it's you. I heard your conversation with Ram Nair. You have always lied to her.

And this time, you went too far! All just to get that bloody pendrive?'

'Can you calm down, Kabir? We are in this together. True, Ram Nair wanted me to get the evidence from her. But I backed off, man! I quit. Tanya was the woman I loved too.'

Kabir would hear no defences. He struck straight at Aman's nose. It started to bleed.

'She was carrying my child. Do you have any idea?'

'Listen, man. Just hold your horses. You have no idea that I am grieving too. But this is not the way.' Kabir was still raging and punched Aman in the stomach.

By now, Aman had lost his cool. Both the men began fighting like errant schoolboys, rolling in the mud and taking turns to punch each other. A small crowd gathered by the time Angami reached the spot. Suri was in the midst of things, screaming incoherently. He seemed agitated seeing the two men fight. Other people were trying to stop them, but the fight was in full swing.

It was when Angami intervened in his assertive manner and threatened to call the police that Aman and Kabir finally gave up, tired and panting. Aman had a bleeding nose, and Kabir had a black eye. Suri was shouting, his arms flailing everywhere. He seemed to be having an anxiety episode triggered by the fight. Ravi Bhansal, the security guard, held Suri by force, trying to calm him down.

'Sahib, Suri can't bear loud voices and violence. He becomes very agitated.'

'Take him inside,' Angami told Bhansal. He noticed that Suri's palm was bleeding and added, 'I think he's hurt.'

Bhansal examined it closely. 'This an old wound but the stitches have come undone a bit. That's why it's bleeding. I will take care of it.' Suri was still murmuring to himself and crying like a child when he was rushed away.

Collecting himself, the inspector turned to Aman and Kabir. 'You two should be ashamed of yourselves. Instead of helping each other and bringing the case to a close, you are accusing and fighting each other like kids.'

'How do you expect me to help a killer?' Kabir shouted.

'You are blinded by your loss, Kabir. You have based your conclusion on a perceived motive and hearsay, not evidence. Ram Nair is an MP. He would have done everything in his power to get the pendrives from Tanya except kill her. There was too much at stake, with the story already being blown up by the media. He wouldn't risk his political career that way, being the prime accused in the sex scandal. Think, Kabir, think. Aman is the one who handed over Tanya's pendrive to me. If he was guilty, why would he do that?'

'How would I know,' Kabir growled. He was still seething.

'I don't need this now. You guys were too close to the crime scene. A few more metres and you would have contaminated it. We are yet to close the investigation.'

'How much longer, Inspector? Just how much? Do you have any idea what this is doing to us? To be in the same space knowing that the other might have killed her? It's harrowing.'

'I get that. But we have no other choice. Trust me that we are closing in on this soon. I need both of you to clean up and come with me for a quick drive to David's house in Khonoma. Is David around? I have a search warrant. I need the keys to the house.'

'Haven't seen him since morning. Bhansal might know. Just give me five minutes,' said Aman. Kabir agreed to the plan too, albeit reluctantly.

'I need to have a word with you in private before we leave, Kabir. Meet me in the canteen once you are ready.'

Angami went in search of Bhansal. He found him in the canteen, cleaning Suri's wound and applying bandages. The young man became agitated again as soon as he saw Angami.

'He has been like this ever since Tanya's death. Not sure why. But something has surely triggered his anxiety. I have been like a father to him ever since his arrival at the camp, Inspector. Suri now needs help with even the smallest of things. He is like a robot. He works in a very skilled manner, following orders to a T, but routine personal chores are surprisingly very difficult for him. So my wife and I take care of him,' Bhansal explained with moist eyes. 'I lost my son when he was twelve years old. Suri is like our adopted son. It's not easy looking after him. You never know what can set him off. He can even turn aggressive on certain occasions. We just always have to be around to calm him down.'

'It's unfortunate that he had to witness this, Bhansal. Do you know where I can find David?'

'No, sahib. He left for Mo village last evening. He said he would be back today. Sir always does that when he needs to unwind.'

'Okay. Thanks. I'd like to have the keys to his home in Khonoma.' Bhansal opened the cupboard and handed over the keys to Angami. 'When David comes back, please ask him to contact me at the earliest.' As he was leaving, Angami had an afterthought. 'Also, Bhansal, do you have any of those old knife sharpeners around?'

Bhansal wasn't sure. Suri began making an incomprehensible sound, pointing towards the kitchen. 'I think he is trying to say that it could be there, Inspector.'

'Thanks, Bhansal.' Angami took out a five-hundred-rupee note and gave it to the old man.

Angami found the kitchen spotlessly clean. He guessed that this was Suri's handiwork. Everything was in perfect order. His gaze fell on the quaint machine kept on a steel tabletop next to the window. In fact, it was fixed to the table. A circular oakwood instrument, with a sort of a wood and iron rotary and an original key. It wasn't very large, so one could miss seeing it. Since Angami had a liking for everything antique, this had caught his eye the first time he was in the canteen. Our cognitive senses are such strange tools. They imprint everything in our subconscious, as our senses perceive even those things that our conscious mind may not register. He had seen Suri sharpening his kitchen knife on it that day. With excruciating perfection, he carved the meat for the steak Angami had ordered. As it was an open kitchen, the inspector had relished watching the arduous process of his food being prepared.

Angami now looked around for something to unscrew the sharpener from the table. He examined it carefully. Nothing outwardly strange. Only Dr Laxmi could see the less conspicuous things. He dismantled it, carefully wrapped it in a newspaper, and walked towards the car. Kabir was waiting there. Angami placed the sharpener in the dashboard.

'What is it, Inspector?'

'I just wanted to ask you a few things. I know you might be reluctant, thinking the answers could put you in danger. But these are things I must know. Just so that I stop feeling like I am losing my mind.'

'Go ahead, Inspector.'

'You are a Khanabadosh, aren't you, Kabir?'

'Superman, you mean,' he said, looking amused. 'Yet I got a black eye!'

'Haha…perhaps you forgot your cape that time!'

'Inspector, your sense of humour has improved tremendously!'

'But seriously, tell me, Kabir.'

'Would it help the case?'

'You never know. Perhaps it would. Or not. Perhaps it would just give me some clarity of thought. You were the one who placed the knife at my door, weren't you? And you were also the one who saved me from the forest. These were not random acts. You were there for a reason. I would like you to tell me more.'

Kabir was quiet for a while. 'Yes, I am a Khanabadosh,' he confessed reluctantly. 'And yet, I couldn't save the only family I knew from a political mob, nor the woman I loved. My parents had no idea where I came from. They thought that I was a divine gift from God after years of childlessness. They found me in a basket outside their home in Ahmedabad. They loved and raised me as their own blood. It was my mother who first saw that I was different, though I myself was unaware. I was just six years old then. One late evening, it began raining outside while I was playing cricket with my friends. Soon, a power outage followed and it became dark. Though I didn't realize it, I was standing radiating light like a glow-worm. Incandescent and periwinkle. The boys were becoming excited and there was a commotion in our locality. Someone told my mother about it, and she came running outside with a towel. Wrapping me in it before anyone else caught a glimpse of me, she whisked me away as tears streamed down her face.

'I could not figure out what had just happened or why she

was upset. From that day on, she watched over me like a hawk. I was never away from her sight. She taught me to never give anyone the idea that I was different or gifted. She wanted me to be as normal as anyone else. And to never ever exercise my special strengths or powers. "They will not spare you. They will come for you if they know the truth," she often told me. I couldn't comprehend her trepidation until much later.

'My mother spent the next couple of years conditioning me to curb my natural instincts as a Khanabadosh. After a while, my inherent powers became dormant. This was her way of helping me survive. So, when the riots happened and my family was killed in cold blood, I was consumed with rage and shame. Despite having had powers at birth, I could do nothing to save them now. I vowed to train myself and regain what I had worked so hard to lose as a child. That is when I started having apparitions and communions with those like me. I started rediscovering myself. I found out that I was born to a woman with supernatural abilities, probably a Khanabadosh herself. My biological mother, Ameera, took birth in a small village in South India. Near Kumbanad, Kerala, to be sure. My grandmother, Beevitha, as everyone fondly called her, was a kind of sorceress. She could heal people and even help them find lost things, people and souls. Yes, she was a kind of divine connection between humans and djinns. She could see things no one else could. In fact, my mother was lost in a forest during an accident after her birth. And it was my grandmother's oracle that helped her find her daughter. My mother was born of my grandmother's ruhaniyat… And I, in turn, was conceived in the same manner. We are not from the seed of men but from that of the divine spirit.

'I have no idea who my father was. My mother was

found murdered one day when I was just six months old. It is rumoured that it was a political conspiracy. My grandmother, a djinni herself, was becoming very popular among the womenfolk, which the village men resented. The day after my mother's death, my grandmother fled the town, fearing for our lives. Not having enough means to raise me, she went from one city to another looking for shelter, and finally ended up in Ahmedabad. Out of desperation, she placed me at my adopted parents' door. Rest is history, as they say.

'My adopted parents died before they could answer who or what I was. They had mentioned Beevitha once. Later, I travelled to Kerala in search of my grandmother. Alas, she was long gone by then. I was shocked to find out that there were a few thousand beings like me. That we were here for a purpose. To save mankind from itself. Today, we are spread across continents, religions, cultures and oceans. But our collective goal is the same. Governments of the world are after us because we are a major threat to their evil, divisive and fascist hegemony. It's an esoteric fight and they will do everything in their power to track us down.

'That night when you were attacked, I happened to be in the forest. I usually go to the woods daily for a few moments of quiet—to relive the time we spent together, Tanya and I. The blue radiance you saw was mine. But that night, I saw someone else. A tall, slightly built man walking towards the area. I quickly hid on top of a tree, between the branches. He was looking for something. It was very dark and hence I could not figure out who he was. He seemed to be searching for something in between the leaves. That was about the same time that you arrived there. He heard you and snuck behind another tree. A second later, you came forward to the exact same spot, bent down and found the knife and began examining it. That's when he lunged from behind and hit your head with a piece of log. I knew I had to act quickly. So I jumped down from the tree top and pounced on him. He was caught off guard and I managed to punch him a couple of times before he ran off. It was pitch-dark, so I could hardly see his face except for a faint silhouette. My priority was to take you to a hospital. So I did not chase him but managed to take the knife for safekeeping. For some reason, I had a gut instinct that the weapon could be connected to Tanya's murder. I took you to the hospital and was with you until you woke up the next morning. The second time I came to your house was to place the evidence at your doorstep. By then, I was convinced of its relevance. My periwinkle hue? I have no control over it. It appears when I am in an agitated emotional state. I have to either run or hide so that people don't see me.'

'Why didn't you tell me all this before?'

'I didn't think you would believe it. Remember how you ridiculed the idea when we spoke about the Khanabadosh a while ago, Inspector?'

'Yes, I was sceptical. I still am a bit. That's how I operate. Until I witness things with my own eyes, it is very tough for me to accept concepts that defy facts and reason. But thank you for helping me out twice. Perhaps this was meant to be. Let's hope we can conclude this case soon. You all must get back to your lives. You don't deserve this. None of you. You need time to grieve. We must catch the murderer.'

'You seem to be quite convinced that it is none of us.'

'I am. I have reason to believe so.'

At that moment, Aman joined them. 'Let's go.'

They dropped off the knife sharpener at the forensic lab

for Dr Laxmi's examination and continued to journey to Khonoma. The two-hour drive thereafter took forever. The heavy rains over the past several days had caused landslides along the way. Navigating the route was rather difficult but Aman's off-roading skills came in handy.

'Why are we going back there again, Inspector?' asked Aman.

'I have a distinct feeling that that house holds the key to a lot of mysteries. Sometimes, walls do speak.'

When the three finally reached Khonoma, they found the house deserted. Angami had taken the spare key from Bhansal. He also had a search warrant from the department ready in case he faced resistance from anyone, mostly David. There were no lights. Entering the house once more gave him goosebumps. He remembered the last time he was here, hardly a week ago. He felt very uneasy.

There was no electricity in the house. The torch lights emanating from their phones led them down to the basement. The air was thick with putrid humidity and rotting food. No one had cleaned the place ever since the sisters' departure. Angami wondered what would have happened to the women had he not found them in time. He shuddered at the thought. Mehr! It was unthinkable.

'This was the room where they were kept,' Aman told Kabir.

'It's so damp, man. The rainwater seems to have seeped in. It stinks here.' The floor was completely wet, and the basement was flooded up to an inch along the walls.

Angami was ahead of both of them. There was another door at the corner of the room, next to a bed. He tried opening it. It was locked.

'Is this a head-hunter's home?' Kabir asked.

'Yes, David's uncle's. He used to be a Konyak chief. One of the last head-hunters of Kohima.'

'This house has a sinister energy about it, Inspector. I can feel it.'

Angami saw that Kabir was very uncomfortable. He had closed his eyes and seemed to be focusing on something. His forehead was twitching.

'Is he okay?' Aman mumbled, inching closer to him. In the dark, with just their phone's torches, it was hard to figure out where they were headed.

And just like that, a purple-blue hue began to take form around Kabir. It was not very distinct at first, but then his aura began changing shades and it was soon illuminating the entire room. Kabir appeared to be in a trance, unaware of what was happening to him.

'Holy shit!' Aman moved closer to Angami.

'Don't be alarmed. He's a Khanabadosh.'

'That is some serious paranormal shit going on. Why is he all purple!?'

'Later.'

Kabir moved towards the door. He turned the knob slightly. And miraculously it opened. Angami was not surprised. Kabir was chanting something. The frequency and the tone of his chants began to rise in a crescendo. It sounded Arabic, or Hebrew. He couldn't be sure. Angami and Aman ventured inside. The room was lit with dozens of LED candles. The walls were full of pictures and paper clippings. The pictures were mostly of David's uncle; there were also black-and-white pictures of King Chingkho Konwang's crowning ceremony as the chieftain. These pictures likely dated back to the 1950s.

There were also paper clippings about the Rohingya slaughters that were rumoured to have happened in Kohima in 2014; the names and pictures of the missing men and women were listed alongside.

At the far corner of the wall, there were more paper clippings. Dozens of reports of Tanya's refugee relief work with the Rohingyas. In the centre, there was one where she appeared to be receiving an award from the UNHCR. There were detailed clippings following Tanya's work.

'Looks like someone was stalking her every move concerning the Rohingyas,' Angami murmured.

'Look at this, Inspector,' Aman said, pointing to reports of Tanya's murder. Every single one ever published. Every press conference that Angami had called. Reports published in local and national news—they were all there.

'This is really creepy now. What the hell is going on?' Aman was aghast.

Suddenly there was a loud noise. By now Kabir was almost hysterical. 'He was here. Her killer was here!' he cried.

'What's he saying? We need to take him out of this room right now, Inspector.'

'In a moment, Aman. Not until we finish doing what we came here for. Be with Kabir.'

There was an ornate wooden cupboard next to the wall. Angami opened it. Skulls of different shapes and sizes tumbled out. There were at least ten.

'What the hell are these, Inspector? I can't stay here any longer. I feel nauseous.'

'It doesn't take a genius to figure out, Aman. These are copycat killings. Like those by the head-hunters. I am quite certain that these skulls belong to the missing men and women

Cry of the Hornbill

from 2014 whose bodies were never found. We just read about them in the clippings.'

Aman couldn't help throwing up. The damp room and the chilling sights had been too much for his delicate constitution. Kabir was still in a trance. He had tears in his raging eyes. His chants were getting softer now. He looked drained.

'This is like a sanctum sanctorum for the hunted.' Angami sighed.

'He was here. We have to find him. He is still on the prowl. He will not rest until he has spilled more blood,' said Kabir, talking to himself.

'What are you saying, Kabir? Who?' Aman queried.

'I can feel his aura. He was here. He is evil. And filled with rage. There will be more. We have to save them.'

'Who?' Angami had no idea what Kabir was saying. Probably *this* was his power—this sense of discernment. To be able to see into the future. Who were 'them' though?

'What do we know about him so far?' Angami said aloud as he ran things over in his head.

'The guy is demented,' Aman exclaimed in disgust.

'Yes, but what else? He hates outsiders. Especially the refugees he likely believes are taking away the land and jobs. Also, he could be part of any of the hardliner political outfits that constantly brainwash people against refugees. He is also lost in the past, aching to revive old, even outdated, traditions. He literally worships Sensi and King Chingkho Konwang. That much is evident from the way the LED candles are placed around their pictures,' Angami noted.

'He has an agenda. Not just against the refugees or settlers in this town or state. But also those people and activists who help them exist. Tanya's murder is testimony to that,' Aman offered.

'Correct. Also, he has perfected the art of decapitation. The murder weapon—that knife—was a dao. Yet he couldn't be one of the original head-hunters. They don't kill at random, especially not on the basis of perceived threats. They are much too principled for that. They were honourable men like King Chingkho Konwang. What they did was part of the war strategy in those days. It was for self-preservation. Never were innocent men, women or children killed. It was combatant against combatant. Such is the legacy and heritage of the head-hunters. But this guy, he's most likely a copycat. He only carries the pride of the head-hunting tradition, without understanding the cultural nuances and historical development of it. As a Konyak, I can discern this. He has probably even been trained in the system. But reality is lost on him. He is deranged enough to eliminate anyone and everyone he begins to perceive as an enemy, no matter the truth. First it was the Rohingyas. Then it was Tanya. There will be others later. If I could profile the person, I am guessing someone in his late thirties with considerable physical strength. Going by the incision on Tanya's neck, he was much taller than her and hence could subdue her easily. I am guessing 5'11" or 6 feet tall. He's very shrewd. Catches his targets alone and is quick with his work. He probably doesn't work alone. May have a subservient accomplice.'

Angami searched the walls again for some clue and then a very recent clipping, probably from yesterday, caught his eye. It was circled in red.

'Government to consider signing the UN Refugee Convention charter. As a token, it will grant INR 5 lakh and a home in Kohima to the three Rohingya sisters Mohsina, Mehr and Zoya, and also allow them refugee status in India.'

'Good Lord!! Let's go, Aman. We need to get back to Kohima. ASAP.'

It was a race against time. It was difficult even for a seasoned driver like Aman to navigate the hills on a moonless misty night. Angami tried calling home but to no avail. The phone was disconnected. He should have given the sisters a cell phone. He hoped to God that he was wrong about their being in danger. For the first time in his life, he prayed sincerely.

◆

The hunter never hastens. He waits for his prey. When the time is right, he strikes.

He did not want to rush things, yet this was the only available time frame. They were easy victims. Too docile and trusting. He should have finished them when he had the chance. In the basement in Khonoma. But his masters had hoped that they would die of starvation, which would look more natural. But fate had other plans. Perhaps it was his ancestors' will that these enemies who were trying to infiltrate their land should die by his hand. He was the 'chosen one' now. As the heir apparent, he felt privileged and honoured to guard his people and their territory. One day, they would crown him as their saviour. Their King, just like the old times. But not yet. There were too many trespassers and transgressors to be eliminated. His hands were restless. It had been three weeks since the journalist's murder. He was insatiable. Revenge was a strangely powerful trigger. It always kept one thirsty for more.

Tonight was a perfect cover. An endless satin sky, breathtakingly noir in its moonlessness, enables our darkest vices. It brings out the most primal in us. It's strange how a blighted curtain of cloud can unashamedly remove the masks that we wear during the day, allowing us to do the unthinkable. In the olden days, he was told, the dark night was a good omen for the head-hunters to stalk and behead their prey. They were less alert in the dark. Tonight was such a night. He was the only one among his peers who had been taught the art of head-hunting. He knew everything. From the planning to the preparation to the chants. If it weren't Sensi, he would never have got curious about his heritage. Yes, though he was never born into it in this life, he was drawn to it. He learnt everything from the old man. After a while he was certain, as were others, that he was a head-hunter in his previous birth, chosen to defend and preserve the tribal way of life. He practised head-hunting when no one was watching. At first it was at the local butchers, and later with wild birds and animals. He never intended to move on to humans. But revenge is a sweet temptation. The blood in his veins raged when outsiders intruded into *his* land. They were like termites, he believed. The UNLF leader had called them that rightly so. He had to do something about it. And he had, with his first victims. That was almost six years ago.

The art of decapitation came naturally to him. He felt like the royal headsman—a sculptor or an artist. He was always robed and ready. It was a sacred ritual. He usually had someone assist him. But after the grave mistake last time, he did not want to take chances tonight. This was his game. He had the most beautiful instrument given to him by his teacher as a memento. An intricately carved antique knife. Nine inches long, it looked like a mini sword. So powerful was it that even holding it in his hands made him feel like God. This knife had belonged to his master. The disciple possessed two of them until recently. But he lost the other one in his last operation.

It was a costly blunder. It wasn't his fault. That time with the journalist...the interval was too short. Hardly 10 minutes. That was a record even for a trained head-hunter like him. It took just 10 seconds for her to be unconscious. And six minutes for brain death. Even in those cases, the conscious mind is awake for a couple of more seconds. He recalled how he called out her name twice. 'Tanya,' he whispered to her, and she opened her eyes, gazing at him. Only to close again. She did it again when he whispered once more a second later. The third time, she didn't respond. It was like a game to him. He liked doing it to decapitated heads. The agonizing fear in the eye of the enemy, at that moment, was indescribable. It gave him a morbid, sadistic pleasure...

Tonight, it was going to be a challenge. There were four of them, including a child. He would have to wait until the lights went out and the potential victims went to bed. It would be bloody. He had to ensure nothing went wrong. It had to be a precision strike. He was already excited.

♦

Qismet was more restless than usual. Mohsina wondered what was wrong with him, and if he was coming down with a fever or stomach flu. It was 10.00 p.m. and there was still no sign of the inspector.

'He will be back. Don't worry,' Mehr reassured her. Yet she had a sense of foreboding.

Qismet spoke in his broken language, 'Ammi, let's hide. We have to hide.'

'What do you mean, Qismet? Please have your dinner and let us sleep soon. You have played a lot today. You are tired.'

He was relentless. 'Ammi, let's hide. Please hide.'

Mehr and Zoya were intrigued. 'What's he saying? I have never seen him so agitated before. What's wrong with him?'

'Maybe he's hungry.'

Qismet was sweating and looked terribly alarmed. He pointed outside. Mohsina wondered what had got into the child. Maybe there were some wild animals close by that he had sensed. He was a very sensitive child. Mahmoud had said never to take his cues lightly. It was always a warning. She drew the curtains and looked outside. It was pitch-dark. There was nothing there.

'Qismet, see, there is nothing outside.'

'I am scared, Ammi. Let's hide. Please, let's hide.'

Zoya intervened. 'Okay, we will hide. You can sleep there. Would that make you feel okay?'

'Yes. All of us. Ammi, Zoya Aapa and Mehr Aapa too.'

'Until he sleeps,' Zoya whispered to her sisters. 'He's upset about something. Let's wait and see. It's just a matter of a few minutes. Let's not agitate him further. Once he sleeps, we too can retire to bed.'

They went into Angami's room. There was a closet there. It was pretty large. The four of them stepped inside.

'Lock the door,' Qismet was stubborn. In the darkness, they could feel the clothes piled up beside them. It was all so claustrophobic.

But Qismet refused to sleep. He was wide awake like an owl, listening to every sound outside. He forbade them to speak. 'Perks of being a mutant Khanabadosh,' Zoya chuckled softly.

A couple of minutes later, they heard some sounds coming from the kitchen below.

'Phew. Thank God. That must be the inspector.' Zoya sighed with relief.

'No, wait. Look at Qismet.' The baby boy was in a trance. 'Remember the last time he was like this?' Mehr said.

'Yes, during the riots. He could sense it even before the event happened,' said Mohsina.

'If it is indeed the inspector, he will call out for us. Let's stay in until then.'

All they could hear now was the deafening silence, along with their laboured breaths and someone's footsteps scurrying up the stairs. Zoya was in a panic.

'Shh…not a word,' Mohsina warned.

They could hear doors opening and closing. Someone was looking for them. He was closing in. He knew they were inside. He had probably been watching them for long from outside. It was obvious that whoever it was, was here for them. They huddled close to each other.

'We can't lose, not now. Not when we have come this close to freedom. Rescue us, God,' Mohsina prayed desperately.

Their killer was now in the corridor right outside Angami's room. 'Ladies, where are you?' they heard a thick accented voice calling out to them, laughing devilishly. He had been inspecting every room to provoke them, feeling sure that fear would give them away. There was no point in screaming because there were no houses close by. The nearest one was a kilometre away.

Zoya was crying by now. 'Try reaching out to Mahmoud, Mohsina. Please.'

'There is no moon tonight. It will not help.' Mohsina already looked defeated.

'Just try. Just try, goddammit,' Mehr whispered.

Mohsina began chanting the verses she had been taught. Qismet was in her lap. She prayed that he keeps them safe.

The Book of Mortality

She chanted fervently in soft murmurs. There was no chance at all, not even a sliver of moon or stars in the sky, and yet she prayed for a miracle. For Qismet's sake. For all their sakes. The footsteps were heading towards the opposite room. It was deliberate. The prolonged torture. Just then, the sisters heard the doorknob turn. The killer paused for a second before he entered. Zoya felt faint. Mohsina was certain that their breathing was loud enough for him to hear. He was just enjoying the game. The rustling of the curtains…a lamp knocked down by accident... It was all by design. He was heightening their sense of fear. It made the victory more valuable to him.

This was it, Mohsina thought to herself. All the years and months they had battled had come to this. She looked at her son, who was also tired now. His three-year-old face looked so mature for his age. He carried with him the burdens of an imperfect world. She had tried hard. But it had come to this. She had failed him as a mother. Her heart felt heavy, and tears were streaming down her face.

A loud thud! The perpetrator was trying to break open the door of the closet, singing an unfamiliar tune. It sounded like a folk song. Nay, a war cry! Mohsina recognized the song. She remembered the stories their neighbours had told them about the head-hunters. This man was here to kill them! He was a head-hunter. She let out a piercing scream from the pit of her stomach. He stood there towering over them with a knife, eyes gleaming as his lips broke into a sinister smile.

◆

'Drive faster, Aman. God!'
'Who do you think it is, Inspector? David? Ram Nair?'

'It's neither,' Kabir spoke drowsily. Clearly, whatever he had gone through in that room had drained him. 'The man we are looking for is not a native. He has cold eyes and a brilliant mind. He has eluded all of us.'

'I know. And soon you will find out too. We need to reach home before he gets to them.'

The men parked the SUV a few metres away from the gate. Angami whipped out his gun. He motioned to Aman and Kabir to enter through the backdoor. It was pitch-dark and, as is often the case when the night is shrouded in darkness, the hornbills were awake and crying. The men heard deathly screams coming from the first floor. The women were in his bedroom, Angami could tell. The three men ran up the stairs and tried to open the door. It was locked from inside. Fighting a race against time, they broke open the door. Thereon, none of them could remember the exact sequence of events. It was as if everything happened in slow motion. It was still dark, with no power inside the room. But they could see the killer's silhouette towering over the group. Someone was on the floor, lying still. The others were in a state of despair, screaming as they scrambled out of the closet. The man attempting to kill them lunged towards the group. Kabir leapt forward and kicked him from behind. The man was motionless for a few seconds and then fell on his knees, still singing the war cry in his menacing voice. The lights came on just then. There were too many details for Angami to process. He wasn't sure if it was all real or a figment of his imagination. On the floor was Mehr, her beautiful tresses scattered across her face, with a few strands soaked in a pool of blood. Her eyes were wide open. A desperate sadness rose in him. Not this time. Not again. He ran towards her. She was still breathing. He tore his shirt and tried to apply pressure on the wound to stop the bleeding. He kept telling her not to close her eyes. She stared back at him with eyes welling with tears.

It was then that they all noticed the killer's face. Kabir and Aman were aghast. Angami wasn't. The past few hours, he had been certain that Nicholas Kent was Tanya's killer. Kent flashed a malicious smile at them before falling to the ground. He was bleeding profusely from a stab wound on the left side of his chest. If they took him to the hospital now, he might perhaps survive. But none of them were in a hurry. So they waited. They waited until the blood on the floor turned a shade of iridescent rust. It smelt of iron and sulphur. The stench of death would get worse with each passing hour until it was etched in their minds forever. It always did. Mohsina was sitting next to the body. Qismet was in her lap. There was a splatter of blood all over her face and clothes. Her hand too was soaked. The child was hugging her tightly.

'It's all over, Qismet. Don't be scared. It's all over now.'

Mohsina turned to Angami and in an impassive voice told him what transpired. 'He came for us. Mehr was the first one who resisted him. I was chanting, trying to summon Mahmoud. As he caught Mehr and came for her with his knife, Zoya lunged forward and bit his hand, so he missed Mehr by an inch. He still didn't let go of her. As for me, I don't know what happened. It was all a blur. All I remember is that I pounced on him, grabbed his hand and stabbed him with his own knife, straight into his heart. On target. I don't know how or from where I got the strength to do so, but something took over me. I know it was Mahmoud. It was dark, so we could see nothing. Yet I knew exactly what I was doing. A force was guiding me.'

'It's over. It's all over,' Mohsina repeated, finally breaking down. 'I may not be able to get the freedom I have always longed for. They may convict me and put me behind bars. Even deport me. But at least my sisters and my son can make a future for themselves. I know you will take care of them, Inspector. After all this, you must.'

Angami hugged her. 'Nothing's going to happen. This was in self-defence. And you have all of us as witnesses. Don't worry.'

At the break of dawn, when the sky was still and all was quiet, Nicholas Kent finally took his last breath. His pulse stopped. It took him five hours to give up the fight with his body. 'He was a determined guy,' Aman said, finally sighing with relief.

'A psychological profiling will give us more insights about what haunted him. He believed himself to be a Konyak. In his heart and soul, he was one. The transformation must have happened when he came to India to work on that project with David's uncle. His undying loyalty to his perceived heritage and territory was what drove him to all this madness. I saw a few bottles of chlorpromazine and haloperidol in his tent when I visited him the other day. These drugs are used to treat schizophrenia and dissociative identity disorder.'

'And all this time I was thinking it was David! He seemed to have the right motive and was hardly around. And I could sense a very strong aura at his uncle's place. I was so convinced it was him,' Kabir said.

'Kent was very clever. He told us a narrative that would have us assuming it was David. Remember, Kent too had access to his uncle's house. He forced Suri into being an unwilling witness. The shape of the scar on his palm is from the same weapon used on Tanya. Kent must have accidentally slashed him during the incident. I was just running through my earlier conversation with him, and it struck me that Nicholas knew that I had found the dao without my even mentioning the same to him. Also, he is left-handed. There was a picture of him at Zahira's home in Delhi holding the very same dao in his left hand. The first thing that Dr Laxmi had ascertained was that the killer was a leftie. From then on, I just connected the dots and was certain. Nicholas Kent was my only suspect.'

'But why would David starve these women for a week if he wasn't involved too?' Aman interjected.

'That was a misunderstanding, I think. He had stocked up supplies for them. But because of the incessant rain, everything got destroyed in the basement. He didn't know that. Or so I think. Plus, there was the travel prohibition for all of you. David was more worried about how Tanya's murder was affecting the reputation of the camp. He was devastated that such a horrendous thing happened there. He was more preoccupied with that. Kent would have eventually got to them in Khonoma, but for some reason that didn't happen. And we found them before that.'

By the time the ambulance and the paramedics arrived, Mehr had lost consciousness completely. The night's events had shocked her into oblivion. Angami accompanied her to the hospital. Zoya and Mohsina were escorted to the police station along with Kabir to file an FIR. And Aman went to the mortuary with Kent's body. Samples were sent to the forensic lab for fluid analysis and comparison. The body was to be kept there until the autopsy was over.

Angami later called Dr Laxmi and went over the case details with her. It turned out that Kent's DNA matched exactly with the samples they had retrieved from the crime scene. The body would be sent to Kent's family in Amsterdam after the autopsy and all legal formalities were completed. A lot of paperwork was pending, but Angami was relieved that everything was over and for once it didn't end tragically.

All Angami wanted now was to go on a vacation somewhere! Hell, he could even get married! He looked at the sedated Mehr and held her hand. Hope was such a beautiful thing.

∞

Epilogue

You, with hazel eyes and skin as dry as the parched earth,
What do you run away from?
The loss of a house burnt down to ashes
A body brutally violated
Or a lover killed, or a son blinded by the pellet gun?
What horrors live within your shadows?
The sea that almost drowned you
The marshes that tried to engulf you
Or the hunger that haunted you?
Yet you remain unwavering
Crossing these seas, marshes and wastelands
A vessel channelling the expanse
To reclaim your lives.
You came to us, the land of the free
With folded hands
Asking not much, except to let you live.
For a while, just for a while, you cried.
The echo of your loss
Still resonates in our ears.
And we, the people of India,
Honour your colossal spirit.
You are one of us now.
You are one of us.

The Minister of External Affairs recited Tanya's verses at the Geneva Convention on human rights and the status of refugees. Millions watched with pride as member nations gave a standing ovation to the lady minister. For the first time, India signed the 1951 Refugee Status Convention and the 1967 Refugee Status Protocol.

The minister thanked the thousands of activists, journalists and politicians who had worked towards realizing this. 'India, the land of Gandhi and Siddhartha, the Ramayana and the Mahabharata, has always worked for the progress of humankind with compassion and tolerance. It is a matter of pride for us to be elected to the council of member states with the UNHCR. History will judge us kindly, as we stand tall in the annals of the human rights and refugee resettlement programme,' she stated.

Thousands of acres of land were allocated for temporary shelters to be built for the Rohingya refugees, until a more permanent solution was formulated with Bangladesh. She thanked and mentioned Tanya Singh, the photojournalist who had worked relentlessly with the MEA and the UNHCR for this to happen. She laid down her life for this very reason, the minister said.

The drug and sex trafficking sting operation tapes were also released around the same time. Zahira, Kabir and Aman worked unabated with major media outlets. It took a lot of negotiations and some arm-twisting to convince them to release the tapes for public access. No one wanted to take on those in power. But finally, when the judiciary took over, the matter reached a crescendo. Ram Nair was arrested. He was made the scapegoat, while others were let off scot-free. Non-bailable arrest, it was reported.

Epilogue

Those who loved Tanya cheered on, and those for whom her loss was irreplaceable watched with tears in their eyes. And then there were others of a different kind: the xenophobes, cultural vigilantes and far-right hyper-activists. This was a blow to their regional aspirations. There were other, less biased critics too. According to them, opening doors to foreign refugees meant undermining an already-dilapidated system with no jobs, and further competition for the citizens to fight to survive. *He* was one such mourner. His losses were of a different kind: honour, territory, heritage, opportunity.

Sitting alone at the bar, he watched from a corner as the drama unfolded before him on TV. His anxiety only aggravated the rashes he had developed the past couple of days. Stress did that to him. No movement or revolution stops with the death of one person. It lives on. Revolutionaries create versions of themselves so that the fight goes on. It wasn't over. Not by any stretch.

David drank his vodka in relative calm as the war cry only grew louder in his mind.